CW01085916

For

Zachary and Georgina.

There are no illustrations in this book, create the pictures in
your imagination, and let it run wild and free.

Love Daddy.

This book is the sole property of Christopher Frost.

No unauthorised copies or performances of this work are

allowed

ISBN - 9781008996038

9 781008 996038

MILO SWAN AND THE GREAT DIAMOND HEIST

CHRISTOPHER FROST

Chapter 1 - Milk

4:59am.

The warm sun is rising into the sky, sweeping over Little Acton. A milk float buzzes almost silently through the streets. Mr Lactose thinks he is probably the luckiest man in the world, as he pops from house to house, delivering the glass bottles of milk. Mr Lactose is a short, round man. He is completely bald, which makes him look even rounder, and has the most magnificent moustache. Imagine the sort of moustache a ringleader for a circus would have, thick and brown which curls up at the ends. He had little creases around his twinkly dark eyes, which made him look like he was always smiling. He quietly hums a cheerful tune to himself, as he drops off his deliveries, his next delivery is number 47 Pleasant Crescent, and it is here, our story begins.

5:00am

BUZZ, BUZZ, BUZZ goes Mrs Swan's alarm, as she springs out of bed.

"Come on everyone, wakey wakey, rise and shine." She says as she bounces towards the mirror, and begins to put on her make-up. "Must look prim and proper that's what I always say isn't it dear?"

"Yes dear" groans Mr Swan's voice from under the duvet.

"Wakey, wakey Milo" yells Mrs Swan into the next room

Milo Swan yawns loudly, looks at his clock and rolls over, pulling the pillow over his head.

"I hope you are getting up Milo Swan, and getting yourself prim and proper for the day ahead."

"Yes, Mother" groans Milo.

Milo Swan rolls out of bed, thudding on the floor. He opens up his wardrobe. Inside there are 7 of the whitest white cotton shirts you have ever seen, and 3 black and white pinstripe suits.

"Milo Swan are you dressed yet?" comes Mrs Swan's voice

"No Mother, I've only just got out of bed."

"Come on" says Mrs Swan popping her head around his door.

The transformation between a waking up Mrs Swan and Mrs Swan after she has put her make up on is incredible. You would never believe that they are the same person. Mrs Swan has done her make up routine so many times it takes her no time at all to get it all on. First she makes her face a strange shade of orange, then she puts on some glittery sparkle, some pink lipstick, puts her hair up on her head like a whippy ice cream, and glues fake eyelashes on before smothering them with thick black mascara.

"Come on Milo Swan… Some of us are ready already"

"I'm going as fast as I can Mother!"

Mrs Swan ran down the stairs, took a deep breath, and opened the front door. Grabbing the milk from outside, her eyes darting back and fourth in panic, before slamming the door and running into the kitchen to put it into the fridge. This was quite a normal routine for Mrs Swan.

Mrs Swan was agoraphobic. Milo wasn't entirely sure what this meant, but he knew his Mother got very worried and a little scared if she had to see other people that didn't live with her. She didn't leave the house unless she absolutely had to, and could get very upset if anything didn't go quite the way she expected it to.

Mrs Swan's fingers slipped a little and the bottle of milk fell through her hands and hurtled towards the tiled kitchen floor. The bottle crashed into hundreds of pieces and milk exploded all over the place. Mrs Swan was horrified, and burst into tears, her mascara making black splatter down her face.

Mr Swan ran down the stairs.

"Are you okay dear?" Mr Swan panics "Oh, don't get upset, there's no need to cry over spilt milk dear, that's what they always say!"

Mrs Swan threw herself into Mr Swan's arms, blubbing into his chest.

Milo Swan made his way down stairs and came and joined the cuddle. He was now wearing his pinstripe suit and white cotton shirt. He must have been the smartest 10 year old boy in the whole wide world.

Mrs Swan looked up at her son, and started crying even more hysterically.

"Oh, Milo Swan, look at you, you look neither prim nor proper."

Milo looked down at his perfect suit and perfect shirt, bewildered at what wasn't prim or proper.

"Your hair" shrieked Mrs Swan, pointing frantically at Milo's head.

Milo Swan may well have been the smartest dressed boy on the planet, in fact he didn't mind dressing in the suit if it kept his mother happy, but the one thing that was entirely untameable was his hair. Mrs Swan had tried everything to get Milo's hair to sit down on his head, and nothing ever worked. When she brushed it down, it stuck back up. When she put gel on it, it went spiked up. When she cut it, it grew back overnight. Literally nothing seemed to get Milo's hair to sit down on his head.

Mrs Swan stopped sobbing and began tiptoeing through the milk towards her son, carefully avoiding the broken shards of glass.

"Milo Swan, you look like you've been dragged through a hedge backwards – that's what I always say isn't it dear?"

"Yes Dear" said Mr Swan, getting on to his hands and knees and beginning to mop up the milk.

Mrs Swan, opened up one of the cupboards and pulled out a hairbrush in one hand and a bright pink bottle in the other. Written in white sparkly letters on the bottle were the words:

Penelope Pompadour's Super Strength Ultra-Hold Hairspray!

"This is a brand new Hairspray." Smiled Mrs Swan, whilst shaking the can frantically.   "Penelope Pompadour says it's the world's strongest hairspray."

A sweet smelling cloud surrounded Milo's hair, as Mrs Swan began brushing. Milo coughed a little at the smell, and winced as the brush ripped through the tangles in his hair. He was about to ask his mother to stop but as the cloud began to clear he could see his mother's face again, it was still covered in blobs of mascara, where her tears had been, but there was something new, that there hadn't been before that morning. A smile.

Mrs Swan grabbed a small mirror out of the cupboard, and showed Milo his hair. It was sat down on his head in a perfect side parting. Mrs Swan threw her arms around Milo squeezing him tightly. Milo liked it when his

Mother was happy, it made him feel happy too, even if he wasn't too keen on this new hair style.

"Do you know what I need Milo Swan?" asked Mrs Swan.

"A cup of tea mother?" replied Milo, Mrs Swan always needed a cup of tea, whenever anything slightly unplanned happened.

"Yes, Milo Swan, a cup of…" her voice trailed off. Her smile began to waiver. Her eyes began to fill back up with tears.

Milo didn't know what was wrong with his Mother but something had set her back off again. She explained through her sobs, waving her arms about chaotically.

"I can't have tea, Milo Swan, there's no Milk, and without milk, tea simply can't exist!" She began hysterically blubbering with tears again, and hugged Milo tightly.

Mrs Swan eventually stopped blubbing, and went back upstairs to make herself look 'prim and proper' again. Mr Swan cleaned up the milk, all the bits of broken glass, and started making Milo a big breakfast.

"A man can't go to work on an egg. That's what they always say!"

Milo wasn't entirely sure he knew what this meant. But he did know that when his Father mentioned eggs at this time in the morning he was going to cook a huge breakfast.

"A Breakfast to rule them all!" Announced a smiling Mr Swan, grabbing a frying pan out of the cupboard.

Mr Swan was a tall, skinny man. So far today he hadn't managed to get himself dressed. In fact he seemed to spend most days in his pyjamas. They were white with blue stripes which made him look even taller and even skinnier than he actually was. His hair stuck up all over the place, and Milo often wondered why he didn't get the same 'prim and proper' treatment that his Mother seemed obsessed with giving him. Despite being a little scruffy, he was a lovely man, and seemed to be the only person on the planet ,other than Milo himself, who was able to calm down Mrs Swan if she had one of her neurotic episodes. Mr Swan told terrible jokes, but Milo liked them, they made him smile.

Mr Swan got Milo to help him with breakfast.

"Mushrooms Milo... These will make you into a fun guy! Get it!" joked Mr Swan as he threw some mushrooms into the pan.

"Boo!" Shouted Mr Swan at an egg as Milo passed it to him. "This one will be Terri-fried" he said cracking it into the pan, whilst laughing to himself.

"This bread, I found in a cage." Said Mr Swan very seriously to Milo, as he put two slices of bread into the toaster.

"Really, Dad?" said Milo shocked.

"Yes… It was bread in captivity" He said snickering to himself.

"Did I tell you the joke about the sausage Milo?" Asked Mr Swan, tapping his chin, whilst trying to remember…

Milo looked at his Dad, trying to remember if he had in fact heard a joke about a sausage.

"Probably not… It's the wurst!" Mr Swan was now laughing quite uncontrollably , and continued with his terrible jokes until he had finally finished breakfast.

"Breakfast is the most important meal of the day, that's what they always say!" said Mr Swan as soon as he managed to stop laughing and he served up Milo's gigantic breakfast. Milo shovelled the food into his mouth. His Dad really did make the very best breakfasts.

Halfway through his first sausage Mrs Swan appeared at the kitchen door, she was wearing a bright yellow dress with a thick green belt around her waist, with matching yellow pointy high heeled shoes, and a yellow hat, that looked a little like a small satellite dish.

"I'm back prim and proper" she said smiling, before taking a deep breath, her eyes going very wide and announcing triumphantly "Today we are going to go out" She paused, before dramatically adding "to buy some milk."

Chapter 2 – Pleasant Crescent

Milo and Mr Swan, both stood for a couple of seconds wondering if they had heard Mrs Swan correctly. As I said earlier, Mrs Swan was Agoraphobic. Milo had never know her volunteer to leave the house before by choice, and yet here she was packing a handbag with just about everything she could ever need. Milo could already see that it had all her make-up in it, and she was now grabbing the pink bottle of hairspray and mirror. She picked a jar up from the window ledge which was filled with coins, and emptied it into her bag.

"To pay for the milk dear." She said to her aghast husband. "Don't just stand there staring at me like a rabbit looking at a carrot, why don't you go and get ready?"

Mr Swan made his way up the stairs and to his wardrobe. Unlike Mrs Swan and Milo Swan's wardrobe, it wasn't quite as tidy. He pulled on an old pair of slightly ripped, bright blue jeans, and a creased white T shirt. He looked in the mirror, and gave his hair a quick brush... Not that it mattered, Milo had certainly inherited his hair from his Father's scruffy locks, and there was very little that Mr Swan could do to get his hair to sit down on his head.

"It'll do" said Mr Swan to himself, before coming back downstairs again "Right are we all ready to go?"

"Yes" replied Milo.

"I'm as ready as I'll ever be." Said Mrs Swan breathing deeply and appearing out of the lounge, her handbag bulging.

Mr Swan opened the front door.

Pleasant Crescent was a lovely little street in the village of Little Acton. There were little white fences around everyone's front gardens, perfectly pruned topiary trees, today the sky was blue, and the sun was shining down, whilst a gentle breeze touched the Swan families skin. Mrs Swan had picked a fantastic day to leave the house.

Mr Swan looked at his wife, who he could tell was a little uncomfortable, and then looked at Milo.

"Why don't we tell Milo about how we came to live here?" Mr Swan said to Mrs Swan.

Mrs Swan had a little smile grow across her face.

"Oh yes" she began.

"It was thirteen years ago, and Milo Swan you were nothing but a twinkle in your Father's eye, that's what I always say isn't it dear?"

"Yes dear"

"Your Father lived in Metro City, whilst I was living here in Little Acton. It's amazing really that we even met one another. One day I went to the city for a little shopping trip, well you know how I am with my clothes! Anyway I started shopping and suddenly I got a little lost, I knew that I had to get back to the train station for a certain time, otherwise I would never manage to get back home that day, and I started to feel a little bit dizzy. I wasn't used to the hustle and bustle of it all, you know what it's like here in Little Acton, it's very quiet, and the city has all the bright lights, throngs of people, and gigantic buildings everywhere. Anyway I'm really very worried that I don't really know where I am, so I sit down on a bench, because I was worried that I might fall over. I sat there and took a few deep breaths, and there was this man sat next to me."

"The most handsome man she had ever seen, wasn't it dear?" interrupted Mr Swan.

"Hmm... Well, you were kind and nice to me. You asked me what was wrong and bought me a bottle of water. Anyway, I had about ten minutes at this point to get back to the train station."

"But we were at least a twenty minute walk away from the station." Mr Swan butt in again "Your mum was frantic with worry when I told her that. Luckily I had my car not too far away."

"My Hero" said Mrs Swan looking deep into Mr Swan's eyes.

"And so all I did was what anyone would have done, I asked if you wanted a lift home. After all it's not that far from Metro City to Little Acton. And I never returned to Metro City did I dear?"

"No, Dear" Replied Mrs Swan.

Mr Swan continued "Then we had to find somewhere to live, we looked all over Little Acton before we found 47 Pleasant Crescent. Oh there were some horror stories. There was Fluorescent Crescent, but it was too bright it gave me a headache. Depressant Crescent, far too dismal, it made me feel sad. Adolescent Crescent but we found everyone who lived there was much younger than us. Present Crescent I just couldn't see a future in it. Pheasant Crescent seemed to be overrun by birds."

Milo wasn't convinced that these were real places.

"But then we found 47 Pleasant Crescent didn't we dear?" interrupted Mrs Swan, much to Mr Swan's disappointment who seemed to have a whole list of other crescents to go before getting to Pleasant Crescent.

"Yes, Dear" he smiled, "and we've been here ever since."

The Swan family walked up to the main road towards the bus stop.

"But I can't go on the bus." Said Mrs Swan looking fearful.

"No problem Mother," smiled Milo "We can just walk to the shops, can't we Dad. It's a lovely day."

"Of course we can." Replied Mr Swan.

And so off they went walking down the pavement of the main road, on that lovely, quiet and peaceful day, towards the shops. Mr Swan and Milo reassuring Mrs Swan, whilst Mr Swan made jokes about anything he could. Everything was perfect, until something unusual happened, but to understand exactly what happened next, you must first understand what happened just fifteen minutes before the Swan family opened their front door. All the way in Metro City.

Chapter 3 – The Great Diamond Heist

An excruciatingly ear-piercing alarm rang out throughout the jeweller's quarter of Metro City, the birds flew away in shock, but the entire street stood still. The noise in question came from 'Paragon's Diamond Emporium', although there was not a broken window, or any signs of forced entry in sight. Another alarm next door at 'Eternity Jewellers', then across the road in 'Prestigious Gold'. Within a matter of minutes every shop in the entire street was screaming out to the world, and yet, if you were standing on the street watching, there was nothing happening whatsoever. No master criminal leaving with a sack over their shoulder. No smashing bricks through windows to break into the shops. It was entirely still. Just the awful noise of alarm, after alarm, after alarm.

Within a few minutes however the street was buzzing, blue flashing lights reflected off the shop windows like disco lights, and police cordoned off areas with blue and white tape. A News reporter stood in front of the tape. She wore a black suit, white shirt and had short pillarbox red hair in a bob. She was holding a microphone, she spoke quickly and excitedly trying to make herself heard above the noise of sirens and alarms.

"This is Fay Queues." She bellowed into her microphone whilst officially staring down the lens of a large camera.

"Reporting from The Great Diamond Heist for Metro City news. More on this story as it unfolds."

There were 15 police officers wandering about, looking at the different stores, each one of them looking as puzzled as the next, all of them entirely clueless. The diamonds, gold and just about anything else from the shops had most certainly been stolen, there was no doubt about that, but the thing that puzzled the police officers was that every shop seemed not to have been broken into.

Detective Daphne Cypher was in charge of the case. She was the only police officer not in uniform, and was also the only police officer who was not wandering aimlessly around looking puzzled. She wore a long brown coat, with a thick brown leather belt. She was tall and slim, and had a pointy angular face. Resting on her nose were round turtle-shell glasses, and her brown hair flowed down to her shoulders like a chocolate waterfall.

"Well," she said to herself, whilst pulling a small notepad out from her pocket "If nobody broke into the jewellers, then they must have already been inside. Problem is, how does someone manage to get inside each of the jewellers, without leaving the one before? Unless there is more than one person behind it all, a whole team of people, but if there was then someone would have seen them, and there is still not a trace of anyone. Not a single trace at all." She looked up from her notepad, and shouted to her fellow officers.

"RIGHT YOU LOT, GATHER ROUND,"

The other officers, jumped to attention and followed the instructions.

"My guess is the thief, or thieves are nowhere near here. If you had just managed 'the great diamond heist', without leaving even the tiniest morsel of evidence you'd be long gone by now. I don't think they'll even be in the city, my best guess is that they've gone to that funny little village down the road... what is it called? "

Although not another police officer dared to admit it, they were all a little terrified of Detective Daphne Cypher. She was the youngest police officer to become a detective, when she talked people listened, but it was very rare that anyone ever spoke back to her. This frustrated Daphne as the reason she had asked the question was she couldn't remember the name of the village. Fortunately for her there was a new member on the force, PC Sydney Harbour.

Sydney was the entire opposite of Daphne, Sydney had short blonde hair, which stuck up a little on top. She was much broader than Daphne and had a round smiley face, and of course, unlike Daphne she wore a navy blue police uniform.

"Do you mean Little Acton? It's my home town?" Sydney said smiling.

"Fantastic" replied Daphne walking towards a police car "Well, you won't mind giving me a guided tour then?"

To say Sydney was excited would be a massive under-statement. She had butterflies in her stomach, she had always looked up to Daphne, and now had the chance to work with her.

Daphne started the engine of the police car and looked at Sydney.

"I hope you have a notepad, because as we drive, we are going to try and get a bit of a profile of the criminal mas-termind, or masterminds behind all of this." Said Daphne sternly.

"You think it was more than one person?" asked Sydney surprised.

"I'm almost sure of it" replied Daphne " how would a single burglar be able to get from one shop to the next, without ever leaving the first. It's a riddle wrapped in a mystery."

"Hmm…" Thought Sydney before adding "What I can't work out is what the motive would be."

Daphne slammed on her breaks, pulled over the car and stared at Sydney. Slowly, as though talking to a total idi-ot she said

"You can't work out the motive for stealing a whole load of the most precious diamonds, gold and most valuable jewellery in the city is? Isn't it obvious? The pure value of it is worth millions."

Sydney didn't appreciate being spoken to in such a way, rolled her eyes and stared back at her superior, before speaking slowly back to her.

"It seems obvious doesn't it? To sell it."

Daphne nodded.

"But I don't think that's the reason to do it." Sydney's mouth curled up a little at the corners.

"Like you say, whoever has done this has got to be a criminal mastermind, yet right now they have got everything from all those shops."

"Go on." Said Daphne, whilst she restarted the car and began driving again out of Metro City.

"Well its everything isn't it," continued Sydney "if you steal a single diamond, I guess you can shift it fairly easily, but everything, the entirety of every jewellers in The City, well it becomes too hot to handle. Don't you think? I'm just saying, no-one in their right mind would buy all that stuff right now, so I don't think they've stolen it all just to resell it."

"It's a good theory," said Daphne "write that down."

Thy continued driving in silence out of Metro City, with just the police radio crackling with various officers reporting on The Heist back in the Jewellers Quarters, as they made their way towards Little Acton.

It was only a short drive from Metro City to Little Acton, but it was certainly an interesting one. Driving alongside the Metro City River, Sydney looked out of the window at the eclectic mix of historical architecture and towering glass skyscrapers. There were ornate bridges over the river, which were plated with incredible gold statues. Before long the river snaked off, and the buildings turned to hundreds upon thousands of houses, tightly crammed together.

The Radio Crackled. A faceless officer's voice timidly spoke out over the radio.

"Detective Daphne, Can you hear me? Over."

"Loud and Clear, over" Replied Daphne.

"We think we've found something in common with the all of the crime scenes, over."

"Notepad, ready Sydney, this could be important."

But Sydney was one step ahead, notepad in hand and ready to write down exactly what it was.

The radio crackled again.

"Each of the crime scenes has got water on the floor, Boss."

"Hmm… Thanks." Said Daphne, before shooting a look over to Sydney, "Well I guess it means something, but I don't know what, any ideas PC Harbour?"

"No, Detective Cypher. I'm really sorry, but I haven't got a clue."

"A clue is exactly what we have PC Harbour, we just don't know where it leads us to."

The car was past the houses and had driven into the countryside, past a sign which said 'Welcome to Little Acton, please drive carefully'. Driving carefully was not something Daphne enjoyed, so she weaved through the traffic instead. They sped passed a street filled with the shops that the Swan family were heading to. Detective Daphne Cypher sat silently driving, whilst PC Sydney Harbour flicked through her notepad trying to put some sort of clues together.

"Anything?" said Daphne, swerving on to the main road.

"Possibly." Said Sydney slowly emphasising each syllable.

The car slowed down to stop at a red light, whilst a family walked across the road, a family of three, the Swan family.

"I'm just wondering… and I could be wrong, but maybe, just maybe, there is a bottled water factory, just down the road. Maybe that's got something to do with it?"

"Any leads a lead" smiled Daphne, before suddenly pressing a button by the car radio, which turned on the police car's sirens. They whizzed through the red lights, and out of sight.

This shocked Mrs Swan so much that she jumped out of her skin, dropping her handbag with a crash. The police car went off over the horizon as Mrs Swan's eyes filled with tears, and she began to wail.

Chapter 4 -Into the Sewers

As Mrs Swan dropped her handbag, everything seemed to go in slow motion for Milo, as it crashed into the tarmac it was difficult to know what to save. Knowing that his mother was superstitious the mirror seemed like the best thing to go for.

"It is very unlucky to break a mirror, 7 years bad luck – That's what I always say isn't it dear?" Milo had overheard his mother saying to his father before.

"Yes dear, unless you are Mrs Brutus who lives down on Toad Road, in which case you are unlucky if you are the mirror." Joked his father back.

Mrs Brutus was indeed a sight, her teeth (or what was left of them) were slightly brown, and her hair looked like a bird's nest which had been set on fire. She wore nothing but grey cardigans and grey skirts. Her face was covered in warts, which made her look like the namesake of the road she lived on, but Mrs Brutus is another story for another day, right now Milo was sure that the right thing to do was to grab hold of the mirror before it smashed to smithereens.

Milo leapt onto the floor, sliding underneath the mirror, and narrowing avoiding the can of industrial strength pink hairspray as it rocketed past him, a grinning chariciture of Penelope Pompadour seemed to laugh at him as she flew past his face. The mirror was indeed saved, and Milo felt a little victory inside his stomach.

Mr Swan put his arm around Mrs Swan, not worrying about the handbag, but just making sure his wife was okay. If he had have worried about the handbag then the coins wouldn't have rolled out of it. But they did. They rolled straight past Milo, straight past the hair-spray, and across the road. For a second they caught the sun, flashing a reflection into the air, as if trying to catch the attention of someone in the family, and they did. Mrs Swan saw the coins through her eyes, although blurred by her tears, as they rolled across the road and disappeared down into the drains. Mrs Swan gasped, pointing at the drain cover and in a small, broken voice said.

"Our coins, how will we buy milk without the coins?"

The family rushed to the drain cover together to see if they could save any of the coins, but they had all fallen into the sewers. They stood silently looking at each other for a moment, wondering what to do, until their silence was broken by an unfamiliar and very disgruntled sounding voice.

"Ouch" said the voice. It was a deep, gravelly voice, which seemed to come from deep down inside the drain. A bright beam of yellow light, suddenly shone up through the drain cover's holes.

"Who's there?" said the voice.

Mrs Swan was positively shaking, whilst Mr Swan held her tight, looking fairly astonished by the whole situation. Milo took a deep breath.

"We… We're the Swan family." Stuttered Milo a little nervously, "We've dropped our money down there, I don't suppose you've seen it?"

"Seen it?" Replied the beam of light "Seen the blasted money? No I've not seen the blasted money, I felt it though, right on my noggin." The beam of light vanished, but was replaced by the drain cover starting to rattle and dislodge. "Whatcha say you call yourselves? The Swine Family?" said the drain cover, now starting to move a little more freely.

"Swan" Said a horrified Mrs Swan.

"Oh posh" said the voice, as a hand emerged from the drains, "Well my name is Denzel Sludgeworth, and if you are looking to get that moolah back, then you are gonna need my help."

Denzel pulled himself out of the sewers. He was, undisputedly, the ugliest man that Milo had ever seen. He was so exceptionally grotesque that he would make Mrs Brutus look like a beauty queen. He wore a dark green overall suit, which was covered in disgusting stains from the sewers. His finger nails were thick with grime and he looked as though he hadn't had a wash in several years. His face was covered in dirt, he was unshaven and had a single eyebrow which reached from one side of his face to the other and gave him a permanent scowl. His head was entirely bald, except for some long straggly black hair right in the centre of head.

Mrs Swan's eyes were wide, she stared from Denzel to her husband, and back to Denzel again, before quietly whispering to Mr Swan.

"This man is neither prim nor proper."

Milo managed to get his train of thought back before either of his parents, he smiled at Denzel and said

"It's okay, I'm sure we have some more money some-where, we will just leave it."

"No, son." Said Mr Swan, looking the most serious he had ever done. "That's the lot, that's everything, your Mum hasn't got a job, I spend most of my life in my py-jamas, we don't have money to just throw down the drain." He turned to Denzel, "It looks like we are going to need your help Mr Sludgeworth."

"Fantastic" smiled Denzel showing off a gappy grin of missing teeth.

The Swans descended down the ladder into the sewers, led by Denzel Sludgeworth. Denzel jumped off the lad-der missing several steps on the way followed by Milo and his parents. They were stood at the side of a foul smelling river in a circular brick tube.

"It's a beauty of a sewerage system" smiled Denzel, flicking on his torch, to show them the walls.

"Built many, many moons ago. I come from a long line of Sewer people, my father was a sewer man, and his father before that, and his father before that. You know why they built the sewers of course dontcha? Back in the day? The great stink of '58... Oh you can't imagine the smell!"

"On the contrary" replied Mr Swan sniffing the air around him "I think we probably can"

"Hmm..." Denzel squinted at Mr Swan, but ignored him, "Anyway my ancestors built these tunnels, so I know them better than anyone, every twist, every turn, I know every rat by name."

"Rat?" Shrieked Mrs Swan "That's disgusting!"

"Well, they probably aren't too keen on you either love" said Denzel offended, as a Rat ran up on to his shoulder as if to prove a point, "Pipsqueak" he said raising his eyebrow "Now do you lot want to try and find this money or not?"

"Yes" said Mr Swan "Sorry for being so rude, it's just this is all a little unusual for us."

"Unusual for us too isn't it Pipsqueak, it's not everyday we have visitors is it? In fact, where are my manners? Follow me. Before we find your money I'd love to show you a little something I've been working on down here."

And at that he turned on his heels and began to walk fast through the sewers, twisting and turning through mazes of tunnels, whilst the Swan family desperately tried to keep up, before he stopped, and flicked a light switch revealing a large chamber painted red and yellow.

"May I present to you," said Denzel smiling and bowing theatrically "The world's only underground rat circus, sit back, relax and enjoy the greatest show on Earth!"

The Rat Circus began. Denzel introduced each rat to do the most incredible tricks. The first act was a pure white rat called Snowflake, with red eyes, and a thick pink tail it which cycled on a small bicycle around the circular chamber, to a slightly bewildered, but albeit impressed Swan family.

The second rat was entirely black, again with a thick pink tail, called Presto. She did an incredible magic trick, with a red ball, which disappeared, and then reappeared underneath a small metal cup, the swan family were now getting more into the show, and were cheering and clapping.

The third rat was none other than Pipsqueak, who jumped off of Denzel's shoulder, and ran up on to a thin pipe which stretched from one side of the chamber to the other. Denzel, pulled out a drum and began a drumroll, as the rat slowly made its way across the pipe on its hindlegs, like a tiny tightrope walker.

Now, if you followed this pipe upwards, then it would travel directly into the plug hole of a kitchen sink. A kitchen sink in a canteen. A canteen inside a water bottle factory. A water bottle factory which was just about to get a knock on the door, from none other than Detective Daphne Cypher and PC Sydney Harbour.

Chapter 5 - Hair

Knock Knock Knock. Went Daphne on the door.

"You have to strike a little bit of fear into them, Sydney, otherwise they'll give you nothing." Daphne said to her new apprentice.

The door was opened by a tiny old lady in a flowery dress with a purple rinsed perm. She wore small round glasses with lenses so thick they magnetised her eyes to look massive in proportion to the rest of her small wrinkly face. She was pacing back and forth and muttering to herself, at the sight of the Daphne and Sydney.

"Oh Dear, oh dear, oh dearie, dearie me. I always told Baxter the law would catch up with him, but would he listen? Oh no mummy. No-one will find out. Everything will be just fine, don't fret yourself, water is water."

Suddenly she looked up and smiled at Daphne and Sydney, as though just remembering that they were there, and speaking in an almost sing song she said, as though on the phone.

"Hello there, welcome to Little Acton Water, Enid speaking, how can I help you today?"

Daphne shot a look at Sydney, then back to the eccentric old woman.

"You said something about Baxter, and the law catching up with him?" asked Daphne hopefully.

Enid looked shocked and sad, and began pacing again

"Did I? Oh dear, oh dear, oh dearie, dearie me. He's a good boy, he really is. It isn't his fault you see. He's not a bad lad, not at heart. All he has ever wanted to do was to bottle fresh spring water, but you've caught him now. I'll take you up to his office? Please don't be too harsh on him, he's a good boy really."

Daphne shot another glance to Sydney, trying not to smile.

Enid started to walk the police officers through the factory. It was industrially beautiful, with copper pipes stretching all around the place, and huge slowly spinning cogs and gears. Steam whistled out of tiny brass chimneys and the whole factory itself seemed to be alive and it seemed to whir with electricity. Enid darted under pipes, and past great vats of bubbling water, before arriving at a door.

"Baxter" she called knocking on the door "It's the police. They've come for you."

The door slowly opened to reveal a tiny, exhausted looking man. He wore a creased up, grey, ill fitting suit, an off-white shirt and a red bow tie. He had a shock of wiry orange hair on his head, and a pair of thick glasses which seemed to be slightly steamed up and smeared. He looked at his mother, then at Sydney, then at Daphne. He seemed to shrink a little each time he looked at someone, looking more defeated with each head movement.

"You ought to come in." He said lifelessly, presenting the office to Daphne and Sydney with a limp arm.

Daphne and Sydney walked into the office. And sat down on two plastic chairs in front of Baxter's desk. The desk was covered in untidy paperwork, so much so that it was impossible to see the wood underneath. On what appeared to be incredibly important documents were rings of a coffee cup. Baxter wandered over and sat the other side of the desk. The buzz of a broken air conditioning unit was the only sound, in this tiny room, and because it was hot and stuffy and a stale odour hung in the air. At the side of the room was an ancient looking television, and bright sunlight shone through the broken blinds, leaving dazzling areas of the tiny office, where dust floated through the sunlight. The waste paper bin was overflowing with balls of screwed up paper, and the room seemed to ooze desperation and sadness as much as Baxter himself.

"I suppose you know why we are here?" Said Sydney Harbour sympathetically smiling, feeling a little sorry for the little man in front of her.

"Yes" said Baxter staring at his desk. "But you must understand it wasn't entirely my fault."

Daphne snapped "Oh for goodness sake, this is pathetic. How can you say it isn't your fault?"

Sydney cringed a little, and she was sure she heard Baxter whimper as he looked up at Daphne.

Daphne continued to lay into the little man.

"How can you say it isn't your fault. These things don't happen by accident , do they Baxter? Do you expect us to feel sorry for you? Well, we aren't all your mother you know, who by the way is also in big trouble as you obviously got her involved too. To be honest with you, I was expecting someone a little more impressive, than a sniffling wreck in a messy office."

Baxter was now shaking so much that his knee was knocking the desk, and making pencils bounce around on the desk. Sydney shot a disapproving glance at her superior, she felt it was a little harsh!

"Oh please don't blame my Mummy, it really isn't her fault at all."

"Seems it isn't anyone's fault, is it?" continued Daphne, "Well you must have had an accomplice, you couldn't have planned what they're calling 'The Great Diamond Heist' on your own. Look at you."

Baxter looked up at Daphne, a look of confusion on his face.

"The Great Diamond Heist?" he said bewildered.

Sydney looked at Baxter a little concerned "You do know why we are here don't you?"

Baxter looked back at her nervously.

"Because of the water?" he said hopefully.

"The diamonds, the gold, the jewellers quarters of Metro City?" replied Sydney.

"I'm so sorry." Replied Baxter, "But I don't have a clue what you are talking about."

Daphne edged closer to Baxter's face, a small smirk appearing across it, before sternly saying.

"Well then Baxter, why do you think we're here?"

Baxter looked nervously from Daphne to Sydney. Beads of nervous sweat were twinkling on his forehead.

"Well." He began, pulling a grey handkerchief out of his pocket and mopping his brow

"I thought you were here about the water. You see it's not technically, exactly what people think it is."

He gulped a little and took a deep breath.

"Little Acton water has got over 500 members of staff, from myself right at the top, to the cleaners. Each and every person is just as important. Without the bottled water factory these people quite simply don't have a job. I didn't do what I did for myself, or Mummy, I did it for them."

Daphne was getting a little frustrated.

"Yes, but what is it that you did? Why do you think we are here? Why is your mother so worried about it?"

"Well, we bottle fresh spring water ,yes?"

Sydney nodded.

"But, recently well, the springs have got a little, well, dry. In fact for the past three years, not a drop of water has come from the spring, at first I wasn't too worried, we had plenty of pre-bottled water, but as time went on, I realised that without the spring I didn't have a business, and without a business everyone would be out of a job."

He gulped, and wiped his forehead again with the handkerchief.

"One evening I stayed in the factory late, and moved around some of the pipes, it's not an easy job, but I had to do it to keep the place going. Anyway, I found another source for the water. But now it's not spring water."

"What was the source you found for the water, Baxter?" Asked Sydney gently.

Baxter took a deep breath, and looked terrified before quietly saying.

"I'm very sad to say that for the past three years, Little Acton Water has been selling customers tap water."

The room feel silent for a second, but that second seemed like an eternity to Baxter, and then Daphne had a smile grow across her face, and for the first time in that meeting she started to laugh.

"You mean to tell me, that everyone out there buying your 'special bottled water' is in fact just drinking tap water?"

"Yes." Said Baxter looking worried.

"And you did it to keep everyone in a job?"

"Yes." Replied Baxter again.

"That's not why we are here." Said Sydney putting her hand on Baxter's and putting him out of his misery. She grabbed the television remote from the scruffy desk, and turned on the television.

The box burst into life, with a cartoon dancing around the screen. Sydney flipped through the channels before finally stopping.

"This is Fay Queues, reporting for Metro City News, from the jewellers quarter, with an update on 'The Great Diamond Heist'. Police have found a hair in each of the shops, one of them is brown, another grey, one is blonde, and one of them is even pink."

"Great." Said Daphne, wondering why she was finding this out from the news rather than one of her officers. "Any ginger hair?" Daphne asked the Television looking at Baxter's hair.

"Early, reports show that strongly there was no ginger hair found in any of the crime scenes." Smiled Fay Queues through the television as if to answer.

Daphne stood up, suddenly from her chair, switching off the television abruptly.

"Do you know what Baxter?" Said Daphne, pausing for a second and thinking to herself. "Your case isn't the case we are investigating, and I think that quite possibly, it could be said that this conversation, never happened."

Baxter looked at her bewildered,

"Come on PC Sydney Harbour, we've taken up enough of Baxter's time, after all we have a jewel thief to catch."

Daphne was now, more than ever, convinced that there was a whole team of villains behind The Great Diamond Heist, with so many different colour hairs there had to be. The two police officers jumped into the car to return to Metro City, to investigate the new evidence.

Chapter 6 - H.M.S Mini Titanic

Back in the sewers Denzel Sludgeworth's Rat Circus was coming to its grand finale. Several rats were standing on one another's backs, making a rat pyramid, which was topped off with Pipsqueak right at the very top. The Swan family, were clapping enthusiastically, and were so excited by the final incredible performance, that they rose to their feet, cheering and whooping.

"So, did you really enjoy the show?" Asked Denzel hopefully, as Pipsqueak clambered back on to his shoulder, whilst the other rats dispersed.

"Without doubt it was the most prim and proper show I have ever seen." Smiled Mrs Swan still clapping enthusiastically.

"I've always said rats are under rated, check your dictionary it's true." Laughed Mr Swan.

Milo Swan smiled at Denzel.

"I think it was the most wonderful thing I have ever seen. You are wasted in the sewers."

"Oh, well, I'll be thanking you muchly" said Denzel grinning his toothless grin. "Now I guess we better see if we can find this moolah."

They began trekking through the maze of sewer tunnels again, despite the overwhelming smell, the sewers were almost beautiful. Denzel was like their very own person-al tour guide for this forgotten world. Despite his haggard appearance he skipped nimbly through the dark tunnels, and was difficult at times to keep up with on the uneven floors. After sometime Denzel and the Swans arrived at a large pipe, bigger than Milo himself, with an immense amount of water coming out of it, and causing an underground river. The Swan family looked at one another uneasily.

"You're not gonna tell me, that Swan's can't swim are you?" asked Denzel, chuckling to himself with a dirty gravelly laugh.

Milo looked at his mother. She was shaking, and Milo half expected her to break down in tears again, but she didn't. Instead something most extraordinary happened. She clenched her fists and raised her voice high.

"Mr Sludgeworth." She began, her eyes squinted at the sewerman with fire and determination. "If you believe that I am going to get into that water then you are very much mistaken. I refuse to ruin my dress, and I refuse to not be prim or proper. We don't all live in the sewers, some of us have standards, so I expect you to find us an alternative route immediately if you know these sewers as well as you say you do."

Denzel looked a little hurt, and walked towards a lever.

"Alright love," he said defensively, sighing to himself.

"I was only having a little joke keep your hair on." He paused and changed the subject.

"Talking of hair, this waterfall has probably got every person's hair from Metro City in it, this is the shower tube, every time you take a shower a little bit of your hair comes out, rushes down the plughole and ends up down here, it's fascinating really, an underground river which represents every single person above it"

He looked at Mrs Swan, and smiled, but his eyes looked sad. Mrs Swan seemed unimpressed by his revelation about the waterfall. Denzel took a deep breath, and looked into Mrs Swan's eyes.

"Mrs Swan, I may live in the sewers, and not get out much, but I do have standards too. I keep these tunnels in their best state looking, whatcha call it? Prim 'n' proper? I have standards in my friends." He smiled at Pipsqueak, who snuggled up to Denzel's cheek.

"And I have standards in the people I am willing to help." He raised his eyebrows at Mrs Swan, who suddenly felt a little guilty for her unkind words.

Denzel pulled the lever. It was a stiff, rusty lever, and made the most awful creaking noise, which echoed off the walls around them. As he pulled it down the water-fall from the tube started to stop, and reveal from be-hind it a large metal bathtub floating on the water.

"May I present to you," smiled Denzel, once again be-coming a showman and flashing his toothless grin whilst theatrically gesturing at the bathtub with his hand "HMS Mini Titanic, god bless her and all who set sail in her."

The Swan family looked in disbelief at the bathtub, then at Denzel Sludgeworth, then back at the bathtub again.

"You named your boat after the Titanic?" asked Mr Swan in disbelief.

"The most famous boat to ever set sail on the seven seas." Grinned Denzel.

"Yes," said Mr Swan, "but you know what it is famous for don't you!?"

"Not got a clue." Replied Denzel.

Mr Swan looked at Milo with a worried face.

"I've got a sinking feeling" He said.

Denzel grabbed a rope which lay on the floor, which was attached to the bathtub, and pulled it to the shore, before turning to Mrs Swan.

"No, need to swim, Ma'am, today we will travel in style. All aboard!" He bowed down before Mrs Swan, who blushed slightly.

The bathtub bobbed up and down in the dirty water. As Mrs Swan with the help of Mr Swan and Milo, climbed into the bathtub. Next Mr Swan climbed in too, and finally Milo. The bathtub rolled left and right almost capsizing whilst the family got in, before they finally found their balance.

"Now the tricky bit." Said Denzel, running over to the lever, and pushing it back to its originally position. The waterfall came gushing out of the pipe again, pushing the boat speedily down the river. Denzel ran to the edge of the sewer floor, and took a huge leap into the air towards the makeshift boat. The Swan family cuddled up together at the back of the bathtub, whilst Denzel started his descent. Every member of the Swan family closed their eyes, and then THUD. The bathtub jolted back and fourth whilst splashes of water around it slopped inside, but somehow it stayed afloat.

"Hold on tight" yelled Denzel as the bathtub quickly rocked back and fourth through the underground pipes. It speed around corners, and bashed and crashed against the sides of the tunnels.

Milo and his Father screamed as the boat tossed through the waves, but Mrs Swan didn't. She was grinning from ear to ear, her arms in the air, as though she was riding a roller coaster.

"I feel so alive." She called out.

Milo stared at his mother in disbelief, as the makeshift boat continued through the sewers, captained by Denzel Sludgeworth.

Suddenly they were in pitch darkness, Milo couldn't see a thing, he could just feel the wind rushing through his hair, and the occasional splash of water on his skin. He held his father's hand tight, as the boat seemed to lurch around a corner.

Suddenly, without warning the boat stopped dead. And the family flew forwards into Denzel, and all four of the unlikely sailors hit a mountain of something hard.

"Hmm." Came Denzel's gravelly voice from underneath them. "Is everyone okay?"

"Yes" said the family in unison.

"It appears we've hit some sort of land, but it wasn't here before... I don't have a torch."

Milo was confused

"What do you mean it wasn't here before Denzel. I thought you knew the sewers like the back of your hand?"

"Oh I do lad, but it's been about three years since I visited these parts. Above this is the thriving fashion quarter of Metro City, and well I'm not a massive one for fashion."

"I'd have never of guessed" said an amused Mrs Swan.

"Don't you two start again" said Mr Swan "So what do we do from here Denzel?"

"Well... If I'm right, and I usually am, then I think directly above this land there should be a drain cover."

"So how do we get to it?" asked Mr Swan.

"I think you already know the answer to that...We climb."

Denzel and the Swan family began to climb, although in the pitch dark it was difficult to know where to put their hands and feet. Mrs Swan's dress got caught on something sharp. Once again Milo expected his Mother to begin wailing, but she didn't, instead she just ripped the bottom of her dress off and left it behind. She seemed to be embracing the adventure.

It was a difficult climb, but eventually they reached the top of the mysterious mountain, and the drain cover above them. They could feel the heat from the sun outside, and muffled voices of the hustle and bustle of the city, although there seemed to be something blocking the holes of the drain cover itself.

"Get ready," Announced Denzel "It's time to go outside."

Chapter 7- Penelope Pompadour's Big Pink Palace

A police siren rang out through the fashion quarter of Metro City, as Sydney Harbour and Daphne Cypher sped toward the jewellers quarter to investigate the new evidence. They whizzed past the flashing cameras and television crews outside a new beauty salon and hairdressers about to open, not giving it a second thought.

The building was designed to look like a giant fairy castle, and was painted bright pink so it stood out against the grey concrete of the rest of the street. A thousand silver sequins hung from each window, and sparkled reflecting the sunlight, the whole castle seemed to glisten almost magically.

In front of the castle was a large red carpet with a huge ribbon at the end, where a host of excited fans pushed and shoved in the excitement that they may be the first to enter. Written above the grand double doors of the castle was a sign with sparkling silver writing; Penelope Pompadour's Big Pink Palace.

There was an electricity in the air from the news reporters outside the Palace. Penelope Pompadour was well known, not just for her incredible hair products, but also for her extravagant lifestyle, and the right photo of her could be worth thousands of pounds.

Suddenly from each of the side balconies of the castle trumpeters dressed like soldiers (if soldiers were to wear bright pink uniforms) began a shrill fanfare, and from speakers around the Palace came a deep voice.

"AND NOW LADIES AND GENTLEMEN, THE MOMENT YOU'VE ALL BEEN WAITING FOR; PLEASE WELCOME THE BARONESS OF BEAUTY, THE EMPRESS OF ENCHANT-MENT THE PRINCESS OF PINK; THE ONE THE ONLY MISS PENELOPE POMPADOUR."

The crowd erupted into applause and cheering, cameras flashed, as the double doors opened, revealing a cloud of smoke from behind, and through it walked a figure.

She was dressed only in pink, with a huge skirt, which puffed out all around her, and made her look like she was hovering through the air. Her top was covered in dazzling pink sequins and crystals, which seemed even more sparkly as the photographers cameras flashed off of them. Her hair was bright blonde, and done up like a huge beehive on her head, and in it was a glistening golden tiara covered in rubies, sapphires and topaz , and topped off with pink roses made from other semipre-cious stones.

"Well hello there everyone." Squeaked Penelope giddily whilst waving a loved hand to her admirers.

"It's so great to see you all here, I never expected to see so many people."

But of course she did, she had personally invited each photographer, and news reporter to come to the grand opening. Penelope smiled the biggest smile, her teeth glistening like stars, at her fans the other side of the red carpet, and walked towards the ribbon.

"Today, is a very exciting day, as I'm opening my Big Pink Palace, but I will also be giving someone the chance to have an entirely free makeover."

At the sound of this the fans the other side of the ribbon started gasping, flapping their hands in excitement and one lady even fainted. It was unheard of for Penelope Pompadour to give away a free makeover, and people in the crowd started waving, and shouting 'pick me, pick me'

She strutted to the rope like a model, and then turned toward her Palace and clicked her fingers once in the air. One of the pink soldiers marched out, holding a pink velvet cushion in his hand, with a silver pair of scissors on it. He presented the cushion to Penelope, who picked up the scissors as he walked away.

Penelope suddenly felt a little wobble, the red carpet beneath her seemed to move slightly, but it didn't put her off.

"Ladies and Gentlemen"

Another Wobble.

"I do heartily declare."

Wobble.

"My big pink palace."

Wobble.

"Is officially."

She took the scissors and cut the rope, closing her eyes whilst taking a deep breath and waiting for the over-whelming cheers from the crowd.

"OPEN."

But nothing happened, there was complete silence.

Penelope opened her eyes, to see the crowd in front of her were in fact not looking at her at all. They were looking straight past her, their mouths open in shock.

Penelope turned around to see what the crowd were looking at, and saw in front of her a man. His hair was scruffy, his clothes covered in dirt, with one large eye-brow which stretched across his face and a rat on his shoulder.

"This carpet is blocking a drain cover, you really aren't supposed to do that." He said frowning (more so than usual) at Penelope.

Then from under the carpet came, Mrs Swan, Mr Swan and Milo.

The cameras from the reporters flashed, and Mrs Swan seemed to forget her worries, or the fact that she didn't look exactly prim or proper, and started smiling and posing for the cameras.

Penelope Pompadour, looked furious, and tried to take control of the situation, again flashing her big smile, but looking more concerned this time. She turned back to her fans.

"As I said, someone today will get an entirely free makeover, who would like one?"

She expected the crowd to erupt into a frenzy of people asking for the prize themselves. But instead they all started pointing, back at Denzel Sludgeworth, who Penelope was trying incredibly hard to ignore.

"Him" shouted a lady at the back. "Give him the makeover."

Penelope glanced at Denzel and then back to the crowd, she looked horrified.

"Yeah, he looks like he needs it!" Laughed another voice in the crowd.

Then the reporters started to join in too.

Everyone was gesturing and shouting to Penelope that Denzel should be the one to get the makeover. This was not the grand opening that Penelope had wanted, but if she didn't do it she would be seen as a failure.

She curled her lips back into position, an icy smile back on her face.

"Very well" she said, scowling at Denzel, before grabbing him by the arm and pulling him into the Palace followed by The Swan family. "Lets give you a makeover."

She turned to her Audience, and smiled her icy smile once more.

"When this 'gentleman' returns he will not be recognisable." She took a deep breath, and turned her back to the crowds outside.

"This could take sometime." She muttered under her breath, before slamming the doors behind her!

Chapter 8 - The Rant

If the outside of Penelope Pompadour's Big Pink Palace was extravagant, the inside was simply overwhelming. The whole place smelt sickly sweet like bubble-gum, and blared out pop hits from the 80s. Every wall had a huge mirror surrounded by glaring lightbulbs, and between each mirror was a gigantic signed photo of an iconic popstar, who's hair had been styled by none other than Penelope herself.

After spending so much time in darkness of the sewers, Milo was starting to feel a little dizzy from the brightness of everything,, his head was feeling heavy, and he realised he hadn't eaten yet. There seemed to be literally no escape. Everything shone and sparkled in a headache inducing hot pink. The hairdressing chairs were black and pink leather, the waiting room contained sofas made from some sort of fake fur that were bright pink, the sinks were pink, above them was a gigantic mirror ball which shimmered more than any mirror ball in the history of the world. Milo found the whole place positively nauseating, and would have asked to leave, if it wasn't for his mother who seemed to be absolutely ecstatic, maybe the happiest Milo had ever seen her. This was the very definition of Mrs Swan's version of prim and proper. but Milo was finding the whole situation difficult to endure.

Denzel had been taken into a separate room to the Swans, and seconds later one of the Pink soldiers had come back out and taken Pipsqueak through a door with a sign above it which read, Penelope Pompadour's Poodle and Pooch Parlour. Although the Swan's couldn't see what was going on in the rooms either side of them, neither sounded particularly pleasant, there were shrill squeaks, and screams coming from both the rat, and the soldier it seemed, in the Poodle and Pooch Parlour. In the other room, Denzel seemed to be groaning in pain and calling out "No" a lot through the salon doors.

"Well at least they will both look Prim and Proper Milo Swan". Smiled his Mrs Swan, whilst admiring the signed popstar posters.

"Mr Sludgeworth is a filthy man, and that creature from his shoulder is not exactly clean is he? I mean whoever has heard of having pet rats? Disgusting. I always say cleanliness is next to godliness don't I darling?"

"Yes Darling." Smiled Mr Swan "Although you know what they always say don't you? Beauty is only skin deep. Lucky for me I've got both in you my love, inside and out."

Mr Swan stared into Mrs Swan's eyes.

Mrs Swan stared back into Mr Swan's eyes.

And they kissed. A long, wet, disgusting kiss, right in front of Milo.

"GROSS!" said Milo, he was shaking, and like someone dropping a mint into a fizzy drink he exploded!

"I AM SORRY MOTHER, I AM SORRY DAD.

I CAN'T COPE WITH THIS ANYMORE.

 IF IT'S NOT ONE THING IT'S ANOTHER.

ALL THIS 'I ALWAYS SAY THIS' FROM YOU MOTHER, AND 'THEY ALWAYS SAY THAT' FROM DAD.

NOT LEAVING THE HOUSE FOREVER, AND WHEN WE DO WE END UP IN THE SEWERS!

NOW WE ARE HERE IN SOME WEIRD PINK PALACE OF TORTURE IN METRO CITY, AND YOU THINK IT'S PRIM AND PROPER.

OUR FRIEND SOUNDS LIKE HE'S BEING TORTURED, HIS PET SOUNDS LIKE HE'S BEING TORTURED, AND SUDDENLY YOU DON'T LIKE THE RATS?

WELL, YOU DID DURING THE CIRCUS!

NOW I'M BEING TORTURED BY HAVING TO WATCH YOU TWO KISSING ONE ANOTHER.

AND TO TOP IT ALL OFF WE STILL HAVE NOT GOT ANY MONEY, AND WE STILL HAVE NOT GOT ANY MILK."

One of the pink soldiers looked alarmed at Milo's rant, and ran through a door, returning with a glass of milk on a velvet cushion.

"For sir, whilst he waits."

"I DON'T WANT THE MILK.

MOTHER WANTED MILK FOR HER TEA, I DON'T EVEN LIKE MILK.

SHE DROPPED THE MILK WE DID HAVE AND THAT'S HOW WE ENDED UP IN THIS ENTIRE MESS IN THE FIRST PLACE.

IT'S RIDICULOUS."

The pink soldier stood a little awkwardly still holding the cushion with the glass of milk on it.

"Sorry, Milo." Said Mr Swan

"Sorry Milo Swan." Said Mrs Swan.

And the three of them sat in the waiting room, listening to the horrific noises coming from Denzel, and Pipsqueak. Whilst the soldier shuffled back awkwardly to the kitchen. Milo shook a little with anger.

"Milo Swan? You're hair has stuck up." Said Mrs Swan routing through her handbag looking for the hairspray. "Let's get you back prim and proper."

Milo turned a shade of red, he was furious.

"IS THAT ALL YOU CARE ABOUT MOTHER? PRIM AND PROPER? I'VE HAD ENOUGH."

Milo got to his feet, and stormed out of the big pink palace, shaking. He started running, not knowing where he was going, just running through Metro City faster and faster. Past the huge crowd outside The Big Pink Palace.

Through Alleyways filled with sleeping homeless people, past mighty skyscrapers. It felt good to run, it made Milo feel less angry, and so he just kept on running, over the roads, through the parks, but it wasn't long before he was entirely and utterly lost, out of breath, and wished that he could be back with his parents.

Milo suddenly realised that wherever he had run too and ended up in was a crime scene. Blue lights flashed from police cars. Tape stretched across the shop entrances, and the street was swarmed with police. In front of him stood a tall lady with pointy features brown hair and a brown coat, and a short, plump lady with blonde hair and a friendly looking face, in a police uniform.

"Hello." Uttered Milo timidly to the police woman. " I think I might be a little lost."

"Hello," said the police lady smiling "I am PC Harbour, but you can call me Sydney, and this is my partner Detective Cypher, but you can call her Daphne."

Daphne shot a look at Milo and her thin lips stretched across her face, in what seemed to be a smile, and although Milo felt bad that he had run away from his parents, he also felt safe to be around the police.

Chapter 9 - The Makeover

At Penelope Pompadour's Big Pink Palace, Mr Swan had run out of the palace but was unsure of which way to go when he got outside in his search for his son, it had started to rain a little. The crowd outside seemed to be getting restless, waiting for Denzel out come out with his incredible, new makeover, and seemed most disappointed at Mr Swan coming outside rather than Denzel and Penelope.

"It's like trying to find a needle in a haystack, that's what they always say." He muttered to himself in a panic, as he crossed the road in the entirely opposite direction to the way Milo had gone.

Mrs Swan sat in the Big Pink Palace blubbing away to herself, refusing to move outside to find her son, and hoping that he would return to her, to her left the pink soldier held a velvet cushion and on top a box of tissues which he passed to her one at a time to try and help her control her tears.

In the next room Penelope Pompadour was still working tirelessly on Denzel, trying to make him look as handsome as possible, despite his own wishes to stay exactly the way he was.

In Penelope Pompadour's Poodle and Pooch Parlour, Pipsqueak was getting to the end of his tether. He had been shampooed, blow dried, had his teeth brushed, hair brushed, tail curled.

"And now, you little cutie." Smiled the pink soldier in charge of making the rat into a work of art. "It's time for a change of shade." Before pulling out of his pocket a candifloss pink dye.

The rat stared in horror at the dye, and leapt off the table, and darted round the room desperate to find the door. The soldier ran after the rat.

Pipsqueak ran under a unit, filled with hundreds of dyes, lotions, creams, and moisturises. The soldier leapt at the rat, but ended up going head first into the unit. Beauty treatments flew off and on to the floor, with plastic bottles crashing off the shelves. The floor began to fill up with the various lotions and potions spreading across the floor. The soldier seemed a little dazed and confused and lost their concentration for a couple of seconds.

Pipsqueak saw its chance to make a quick getaway. It ran across the floor, skidding through a greasy, slippery mixture, and lost control entirely, sliding and spinning like an ice skater towards an abundance of white foam, coming from a bright pink bottle. If Pipsqueak had have been able to read, he would see that the bottle said 'Penelope Pompadour's Instant Hair Growth Volumizing Mousse.'

With a huge splat Pipsqueak flew through the Mousse, sending a cloud of the white foam into the air, which drifted down in front of the pink solider like snow.

Pipsqueak felt his hair shaking. He was tingling, vibrating. It felt like bolts of electricity were spreading out around him. He stared at the pink soldier, who's eyes were getting wider and wider with sheer terror, as he looked at the rat, which appeared to be growing bigger and bigger by the second.

Pipsqueak was feeling bigger too, he looked down at his fur. He was at least ten times the size he was before, and he took a step towards the soldier.

The Soldier screamed, got to his feet and ran out of the door, past Mrs Swan, and out of the Big Pink Palace.

As the door opened the crowd feel silent, and every eye rested on him, expecting to see Penelope and Denzel. Once again they were disappointed as a pink soldier appeared running as fast as he could past the cameras and crowds. There was a collective disappointed sigh from the crowd.

Pipsqueak, slowly strutted towards the open door of the Poodle and Pooch Parlour, and caught a glance of his reflection in the mirror. He looked gigantic, he almost alarmed himself. He edged out of the door, into the waiting room. Mrs Swan stared sympathetically at the Rat.

"Oh Pipsqueak." She said, forgetting her own problems for a second. "What have they done to you?"

The pink soldier looking after Mrs Swan took one look, and ran out of the Pink Palace too, not even stopping to put down the cushion with tissues on it. Again the crowd took a collective deep breath as the door opened, but once again were disheartened by the lack of Penelope and Denzel.

"I don't think they are ever going to come out." Said one man in the crowd.

"He's just too ugly, she can't fix him." Shouted another lady. The crowd roared with laughter.

"I've wasted enough of my time today. I'd stay if I thought the weather was going to get better" Said another putting out there hand to show everyone it was raining " but... I'm off."

And slowly, over a little time, the crowd started to leave. The TV cameras disappeared, the news reporters walked away, and the Big Pink Palace ended up deserted, except for the odd shopper rushing past trying to avoid the rain which was now coming down heavily now.

Penelope looked at the beautician chair in front of her, and smiled to herself.

Denzel made an exhausted grunt from the chair, defeated.

His hair had been made into an elaborate spiky sculpture with various different Penelope Pompadour hair products.

His face had been sucked with a mini vacuum cleaner, to get any gunk out of it, and three different types of face masks daubed on top of it.

Slices of cucumber covered Denzel's eyes, and he had been shaved.

Penelope Pompadour had even managed to get an expensive fashionable suit delivered through one of the back entrances to the palace, and asked Denzel to dress in it.

Denzel looked absolutely incredible, almost like a different person

"Well Mr Sludgeworth, you were quite the project. But I think it's safe to say you are my masterpiece." Penelope threw a cloud of glitter over herself, and checked her lipstick in the mirror. "We are ready to let my, I mean our, adoring public see us. Take a deep breath Mr Sludgeworth, you are about to become a celebrity." She spoke to him like he was a small child, or worse a tiny dog that you could keep in a handbag. "Come along now Mr Sludgeworth."

Denzel took the cucumber slices away and rolled his eyes.

"I don't wanna to be a celeb. I was 'appy the way I was."

Penelope's smile vanished, and she looked sternly at Denzel.

"How could you possibly have been happy looking like… THAT? Listen," She said grabbing his tie and pulling his face close to hers "You were not exactly my first choice of model either Sludgeworth. But you are going to go out there and smile for the cameras, or else." Her eyes shot him a threatening look, they looked cold and angry.

"Or else what?"

"Oh, Mr. Sludgeworth, don't ask too many questions." Penelope's eyes flashed. "You have no idea what I am capable of."

Chapter 10 - Newton Springheel

The clouds became more ominous over Metro City, and the rain became heavier and heavier. Mr Swan had been walking for over an hour trying to find Milo, and was wet through to the bone. His jeans had turned much darker, and his T shirt transparent, but he didn't care.

"MILOOO." He called out frantically.

The amount of people in Metro City seemed to be less and less, Mr Swan first thought this was due to the rain, but he had now realised that he wasn't in the best part of Metro city. This part of the City had large grey concrete buildings towering over him, casting dark shadows in different directions across the pavement. Most of these buildings seemed to be empty, with smashed windows, and front doors boarded up with wood.

Mr Swan felt very uncomfortable A tram rattled over a bridge, behind him.

"I'm the wrong side of the tracks. That's what they always say." Muttered Mr Swan to himself, a glint of a smile flickering over his face, before worry set back into the creases across his forehead.

Way ahead of him the shadow of a figure rushed between buildings. Mr Swan's first thought was that it could be Milo, but even if it wasn't it perhaps it was someone who had seen him.

Mr Swan, ran through the puddles towards the figure, but it had gone. Mr Swan took a deep breath, and sighed. He felt unsafe, alone and worried about Milo.

He was standing between two huge concrete buildings. They were crumbling, and had hundreds of bird droppings down the side of them and squiggles of faded graffiti. Pigeons cooed looking down at Mr Swan inquisitively.

One pigeon flew down in front of Mr Swan and flew into a dark alleyway ahead.

"Oi" Shouted a voice from the darkness "Gerroff, you bleedin' skyrat."

The bird flew back out again looking slightly stunned, and returned to its perch high up on the top of the concrete, and cooed loudly, before pooing down the building.

Mr Swan called into the darkness.

"Hello." Said Mr Swan nervously "Who's there."

Slowly, the figure appeared out of the alleyway.

In front of Mr Swan stood a tall, skinny man dressed entirely in brown rags fashioned into a sort of long coat. His skin was dark and leathery, and covered in wrinkles. Across his right eye was a brown leather eyepatch, but the visible eye was large, bright green, and staring unforgivingly at Mr Swan. He had an untidy, grey beard, and grey dreadlocks cascading down from his head. In his right hand he clutched a loaf of bread, and with his left hand he pointed a crooked, bony finger at Mr Swan, his finger nails were long, jagged and dirty. His voice was a raspy whisper, and he sounded furious at being seen by Mr Swan.

"You're in my part of town. So it's up to me to ask you who's there? Not the other way round. So who are you? And what are you doing here?"

Mr Swan looked down.

"I'm looking for my son." Said Mr Swan sadly "He ran away, and now I can't find him anywhere."

"Oh Dear," Said the stranger a little more gently, and lowering his finger "What's 'is name?"

"Milo." Said Mr Swan, pulling his empty wallet out of his pocket and showing the man a photograph of Milo which he treasured inside. "Milo Swan."

"You a Swan too?" rasped the man.

"Yes." Said Mr Swan nodding.

"Well Swan, let's get you outta' this 'ere rain, maybe I can 'elp ya. The name's Newton Springheel. Follow me."

Newton sped off, bouncing over the puddles like a gazelle into the darkness. Mr Swan found it difficult to keep up, his wet jeans were rubbing against his legs, and Newton seemed so used to the area, that he moved almost like he was on a pogo stick through the urban avenues and alleyways.

"Keep up Swan." Called Newton behind him, his dreadlocks bouncing as he darted between buildings. "I reckon we can find your boy very, very soon."

Eventually Newton stopped outside a grand looking building, Mr Swan trailing behind. This building was crumbling, yet still stood majestically in front of them. There was a huge unlit sign across the building 'The Regal Cinema'. There were black sparkling steps leading up to the grand doorways. The handles were golden spirals which wouldn't have looked out of place in the 1920s. Either side of the doors were two large concrete lions, and beyond the doorways were red luxurious carpets. The building seemed, sadly, destroyed beyond all repair, despite the beauty it may have once had.

"Not this way." Said Newton, running around the back of the cinema. "We use the other entrance."

Mr Swan followed Newton around the back of the building, there was a metal staircase, leading up to a red wooden door.

"Is Milo here?" said Mr Swan hopefully.

"Afraid not Swan, but there is someone 'ere who can 'elp you."

They climbed the metal staircase, and walked through the red door.

The cinema building may have been abandoned long ago, but it was certainly not empty. The cinema floor was covered in sleeping bags, some with people still asleep inside of them. The unlikely pair tiptoed over the mass of sleeping people.

"Try not to wake 'em Swan," Whispered Newton "Everyone needs their sleep."

Some were not lucky enough to find a space on the floor, and had taken to sleeping in the red velvet seats instead.

"What is this place?" asked Mr Swan.

"It's our 'ome, Swan. An 'ome for the 'omeless."

Mr Swan was shocked.

"But there are so many of you. How do you become homeless?"

"Oh Swan, there is a billion reasons for becoming 'omeless. No one chooses to not 'av an 'ome, but let me tell ya somfink, these people are gooduns, there ain't a bad egg among us. 'Omless get a bad reputation, but we ain't all bad people."

Newton led Mr Swan out of another door into the foyer area of the building. There was a large desk, with drink and popcorn machines behind it, and the walls were covered in faded posters of films from bygone times.

"But what happens if they try to move you along?" asked Mr Swan.

Newton gave a snort of laughter at the thought of it.

"That's where Raymondo comes in… That's who I'm taking you to, Raymondo."

"You think he knows where Milo is?" asked Mr Swan hopefully.

"Raymondo knows EVERYFINK, Swan." Smiled Newton "Everyfink." He said, more quietly, nodding to himself.

They walked down a corridor of doors leading to screens, until the went into screen 12.

The room was black, but the screen was lit from the projection box, with hundreds, of tiny screens.

"Raymond has managed to 'ack to CCTV of the whole of Metro City. Every new mayor, or politician who tries to move us along, Raymondo is the eye in the sky for them. They wont move us along, 'cos they know, that we know everyfink there is to know about them. All their secrets. Which also means, if your son is in this 'ere City, then Raymondo will find him quick as a flash."

Mr Swan ran up to the projection box at the back of the cinema, and knocked. The projector was so bright showing the screens that Mr Swan could barely make out the figure inside. As his eyes adjusted, he saw that Raymond was a short timid man, in a red waistcoat, white shirt and black bowtie. Mr Swan realised that this must have been the cinema uniform at sometime.

Mr Swan explained what had happened to Milo, and Raymondo typed into his computer. The CCTV screens flipped across the cinema screen as Raymundo's fingers danced over the computer keys. Eventually the screens stopped flickering, to stop on the outside of an American style diner, it's door opening, and out walked Milo behind two police officers. They got into a police car, and sped out of the carpark, sirens wailing.

Mr Swan's eyes were wide…

"Oh Milo… What have you done?"

Chapter 11 - Tom's Diner

Had Mr Swan had known the whole story of why Milo was with the police he needn't have worried, for whilst Mr Swan made new friends with Newton Springheel, Milo was making friends with Sydney and Daphne.

Milo sat down with PC Harbour and Detective Cypher as he explained everything that had happened. Sydney Harbour munched on a cheese and ham baguette, whilst Daphne Cypher pecked at a pre-made salad. Food crossed Milo's mind again, he suddenly felt starving hungry. Sydney noticed Milo starting at the baguette longingly.

"It's lunch time." She said smiling. "Have you had anything to eat?"

"I've not really had time to, between the sewers, and the bathtub, climbing the mountain in the dark and then ending up in The Big Pink Palace, but I am incredibly hungry."

Daphne couldn't stop staring at Milo as he talked about his adventure. She had stopped eating her salad entirely, and was wide eyed as she slowly took her walkie talkie up to her mouth.

"I'm going to need some science geeks. To test the water." She said seriously, not taking her eyes off Milo. "There is a young man here, and I think he could be the missing piece of the jigsaw."

Milo looked a little alarmed about being the missing piece of any jigsaw which involved so much police tape.

"You don't think I did this... Whatever this is?"

Sydney looked as confused as Milo, but Daphne just chuckled to herself.

"Why of course not, but I think you may have helped us a lot more than you would know, the story of everything could just explain exactly how it was all done. You've not eaten for a little while, shall we take you for some food?"

Milo nodded enthusiastically, and jumped into the car with the police officer and detective, as they sped off for something to eat.

A large white van with 'forensics' written across it shrieked to a halt at the end of the street, out rushed five figures dressed from head to toe in white all in one biohazard suits, with masks across their faces. They each rushed into a different shop, and then seconds later ran back to the van holding test tubes. The street seemed still again for some moments.

Inside the van there was everything you could imagine to test the water, and the forensic police took drops of water from the test tubes in plastic droppers and popped them all on to small glass slides. The Forensic policeman in charge then took each slide, one by one and checked them under a microscope. He fiddled with the twisty knobs at the sides, of the microscope, to focus. Before looking at his colleague, his eyes wide.

"This is no ordinary water…" He said, looking quite disgusted "This is toilet water."

Milo had never been to a restaurant before, and he didn't expect his first time to be with two police officers. They had just drawn up in the police car to a large fast food restaurant. The outside of the restaurant had a huge light up neon sign which flashed with the words 'Tom's Diner' in fancy writing, and there was a low electrical hum.

Although it was only a very short walk from the police car to the Diner, Daphne pulled out a large umbrella, and the three of them huddled underneath it, as they rushed through the car park, avoiding the puddles.

Milo, Daphne and Sydney walked through the large glass doors. The floor had black and white square tiles, like they are walking over a gigantic chess board, and there are tables all around the outside, surrounded by large red plastic sofas, each table had a small plastic tomato on it, and a long yellow squeezy bottle.

Milo had always thought that a place like this would play music from the 50s, but instead it just seemed to be an almost hypnotic chant playing over the radio, over and over again, it made him feel very relaxed, and a little sleepy.

There was a long light blue counter, with a lady sitting at it with half a cup of coffee, and a newspaper, behind her in the corner was a Television, playing music videos on but on mute, so the hypnotic chant didn't fit at all with the videos showing on the screen.

The other side of the counter was a short fat man. He had a red polo t-shirt on with 'Tom's Diner' in white writing on it.

Daphne gives her umbrella a little shake.

"It's always nice to see you!" says the man behind the counter loudly to Daphne. He then rushes forwards to give her a kiss on both the cheeks. "Coffee?" asks the man.

"Oh yes please, and a special burger for young Milo please."

"Why of course" smiles the man at Milo "Coming up."

The unlikely three sat down on the plastic sofas at a table, and the man bought them each a coffee.

"I don't really drink coffee." Said Milo. "I'm not allowed it."

"I'm sure you aren't really allowed to run away from your parents." Smiled Sydney.

"Or befriend a criminal mastermind that lives in the sewers." Said Daphne sternly.

Both Sydney and Milo looked confused.

"If I'm correct, and I usually am, then I would say this Denzel character, is the person who stole all the jewels last night." Smiled Daphne.

Milo shook his head in disbelief.

"No, He can't be. He's my friend." Said a mortified Milo.

Sydney put her arm around Milo.

"She has been wrong before Milo." Said Sydney reassuringly, as Daphne shot her a hardened glance. "Well you were wrong about Baxter in the spring water factory."

Daphne cringed.

"Yes, yes I was. But I have a feeling about this Denzel. You said that you went past a waterfall where he was very excited about all the different hair that came through the sewers."

"Yes?" said Milo.

"And each of our crime scenes had something in common. Hair and water."

Milo's face fell, he had truly trusted Denzel and found it awful to think the man he had trusted to guide them through the sewers was a hardened criminal.

Suddenly from nowhere the man came back with the biggest burger Milo had ever seen. It was stacked high, in a polystyrene container. The man smiled at Milo.

"It's our biggest burger yet." He pointed at each stack.

"Bread. Beef. Chicken. More Bread. Halloumi. Pulled Pork. A Fried Egg. Salad. And Bread. My Masterpiece."

Milo stared at the burger amazed at its pure size, and licked his lips.

The music videos on the television screen suddenly went blank and were replaced with a newsflash. Fay Queues stood staring out of the screen.

"Quick!" Shouted Daphne to the man. "Turn the sound up."

"This is Fay Queues, reporting for Metro City News" crackled the red headed reporter through the television "An update on The Great Diamond Heist! Forensics have told us that they've found toilet water in each of the crime scenes. Dodgy Plumbing? Or a major clue for the Metro City Police force?"

Daphne raised her eyebrows, and looked at Sydney and Milo as if to say 'I told you so'.

Milo looked down at his gigantic burger.

"Suddenly I don't feel so hungry." He said pushing it away.

"You might as well bring it with you. We've got an arrest to make."

Daphne, Sydney and Milo, went back out into the rain to the police car, sirens on they sped out of the car park and towards the Big Pink Palace.

Milo had no idea that his father was watching through a nearby CCTV camera, and going out of his mind with worry!

Chapter 12- Under Arrest

Mrs Swan sat waiting in the reception of the Pink Palace waiting for the return of her son, whilst cuddling Pipsqueak.

The Rat was now fully volumized, and around the same size as a Labrador, and twice as fluffy. He sat loyally by Mrs Swan's side.

The door opened and out came Penelope Pompadour. She gave Mrs Swan a flashy smile, but took several looks at the rat trying to work out what it was.

"Mrs Swan, and your... unusual pet." Smiled Penelope, looking suspiciously at Pipsqueak.

"May I present to you my masterpiece."

Penelope gave a large flourish with her arms towards the door, before glaring inside and whispering angrily.

"Denzel, get yourself out here this minute."

Slowly Denzel walked sadly and solemnly out of the Salon.

He was almost unrecognisable. His face was clean shaven, and he was tanned a glowing brown. His teeth were pure white, and appeared to all be there, his hair was short and smart, his eyebrows were no longer a single brow across his face, but now two defined lines and his finger nails glistened.

He looked shyly at Mrs Swan.

" 'Ello Mrs Swan, do I look utterly ludricrous?"

Mrs Swan stared at the transformation in front of her, and stuttered.

"No, Denzel, you look absolutely by far more prim and proper than I ever thought it was possible too."

Penelope Pompadour grinned at Denzel, grabbing him by the arm and dragging him towards the large double doors of The Big Pink Palace.

"See Mr Sludgeworth, and now it's time for us to meet our fans." She Said grinning. She looked at herself in the mirror, and adjusted her tiara, which glistened under the gigantic disco ball.

Blue lights flashed through the frosted glass of the palace windows.

"The photographers will want a nice big smile from you Mr. Sludgeworth, can you show me your biggest smile?" She asked him again, as though he were a tiny toddler.

Denzel grimaced awkwardly at Penelope, as she flung open the doors of the big pink palace, a gigantic grin on her face.

But the lights flashing through the windows of the palace were not those of photographers, instead 5 police cars waited outside, and at the end of the red carpet, stood Daphne, Sydney and Milo.

Daphne held a megaphone to her mouth, and had a stern look on her face.

"DENZEL SLUDGEWORTH, YOU ARE UNDER ARREST FOR THE CRIME OF THE CENTURY, THE GREAT DIAMOND HIEST, COME HERE WITH YOUR HANDS UP."

Penelope let go of Denzel's hand, a stunned look on her face, before a faint smile flickered across her face. She gave him a sharp shove towards the red carpet

Denzel looked entirely confused by the whole situation he was finding himself in.

"But...I"

"MR SLUDGEWORTH YOU DO NOT HAVE TO SAY ANYTHING, BUT ANYTHING YOU DO SAY CAN AND WILL BE USED IN EVIDENCE."

"You heard them" Hissed Penelope, giving him another push towards the police.

Slowly, Denzel started walking down the red carpet towards the police car. His eyes fixed on Milo.

Milo looked up at Denzel finding it difficult to believe this gentle giant who had earlier shown them the rat circus was now being arrested for The Great Diamond Heist.

Denzel put out his hands as Sydney placed handcuffs on him, and he looked down at Milo, and whispered.

"It wasn't me, you have to find out who did this."

Daphne and Denzel sped off in the car, sirens wailing, and Daphne shouted to Sydney.

"You stay here in case there is any more evidence."

Milo looked up.

Penelope stood in her door way, her face glinting with a sparkling smile, as film crews and photographers descended on the Big Pink Palace.

"There's no such thing as bad publicity." She smiled as a Fay Queues pulled her to one side to explain the drama that had just taken place.

Milo looked further, and saw his mother, sat in the reception of The Big Pink Palace, she was cuddling the ludicrous looking furball that was Pipsqueak.

Suddenly, nothing else mattered to Milo except for the fact hat he had run away.

"Mum!" He cried, and he ran towards her, straight along the red carpet.

Mrs Swan looked up and a smile appeared on her face.

"Milo." She called.

Milo ran and ran down the red carpet, his arms out towards his mum. But then... SPLAT!

He fell straight through the hole that they had come out of with a heavy bump, the dark mountain underneath him which led to the sewers.

Sydney ran over to him.

"Are you okay?" She called

"Yes, shouted Milo, I just want to see my Mum."

Sydney pulled a torch out from her bag and shone it into the hole. Suddenly lights reflected back at her from the sewer, dazzling her and making a beautiful pattern against the walls of The Big Pink Palace.

Milo looked down, to find that the mountain was in fact a huge hill of diamonds, gold, silver, emeralds, hundreds upon hundreds of precious things.

Sydney smiled at Milo.

"Well young man. I think you may have found where Denzel hid his treasure."

Penelope Pompadour spun round, staring angrily at the discovery, before turning back to the new reporter to continue her interview.

Mr Swan stared at the cinema screen in front of him. They had followed the CCTV all the way back to The Big Pink Palace.

"So this." Smiled Raymondo "is what is going on right now. It seems like your son has just fallen down some sort of a hole."

Mr Swan looked both worried and a little relieved.

"Well at least we know exactly where he is, its exactly where we came from, one step forward and two steps back, that's what they always say isn't it. Is there anyway I can help you all to thank you?"

"Probably not." Sighed Raymondo. "See if you can get this place turned into real accommodation for us? Everyone's got to dream."

"I don't think I can do that. It'd cost thousands" Said Mr Swan sighing sadly. "But I'll do my very best." He added with a reassuring smile.

"Go an' get ya son" smiled Newton Springheel.

Mr Swan nodded and left the cinema.

Despite being able to see what had been going on Mr Swan hadn't heard a thing, and the whole situation seemed very bizarre.

So he ran, as fast as his legs could carry him, his heart beating like a drum and the rain pouring into his face.

It seemed like forever until he arrived outside The Big Pink Palace.

Milo was sat snuggled up with his Mother and pipsqueak, whilst PC Sydney sat asking them questions. Mr Swan rushed, past Penelope who was now basking in the limelight, and over to them.

"What's going on?" He asked.

"Oh Dad, it's so good to see you. But it's a long story let me explain."

Chapter 13- Sock

Denzel sat in a small room opposite Daphne Cypher, the harsh lighting shining off his flashy new suit.

Daphne glared suspiciously at his pristine hair and gleaming finger nails.

"I know I don't LOOK like I work in the sewers, that's because that awful woman has changed the way I look entirely." Muttered Denzel.

Daphne Cypher sat staring hard at Denzel, unamused.

"You look like you've just robbed a whole loads of diamonds to pay for your suit, all the evidence says you've just robbed a whole load of diamonds. The Sewers, which you claim to work in are full of the diamonds, the water we found in the jewellers is sewer water, and you even climbed up a mountain of diamonds to get out of the sewers. Yet you say you don't know anything about it."

Denzel looked down, perplexed.

"I'm not lying to you Miss Cypher."

"DETECTIVE CYPHER" Glared Daphne correcting Denzel. "Now, if you wont tell me what I need to know, perhaps you will follow me to your cell for the night, maybe that will help you to remember what happened."

Denzel was taken through a long corridor and up several staircases to a small cell. It was everything he expected it to be. A small concrete room. In the corner there was a toilet. At the side a concrete bed. An opening to outside (which you couldn't really call a window, as windows have glass) with three metal bars across it.

"Welcome to your new home Denzel." Said Daphne, before closing the thick metal door with a mighty crash, and then turning the lock with a metallic clunk.

"Perhaps a night in the cells will refresh your memory of what really happened" called Daphne through the door.

Denzel sat down, put his head in his hands and tears started to form in his eyes. It was true everything pointed directly to Denzel.

He couldn't prove that he hadn't done it, not from inside a cell, he had to rely on Milo.

He looked out through the bars of his window. He was several floors in the air. Even if he was able to escape out of the window he wouldn't be able to get down. He looked around the rest of the room. Before his eyes got fixed to the toilet.

"Where there's a will there's a way. That's what Mr Swan would say."

Slowly Denzel started to hatch a plan, if he couldn't prove his innocence he could at the very least escape from prison.

Denzel sat down on his concrete bed, staring at the toilet. And took off one of his shoes. Then his sock.

He walked to the toilet with his sock and dropped it into the toilet with a splosh.

Then he pulled the chain hard.

The water speed into the toilet, washing away the sock from the bowl, and into the pipes below.

The sock tossed and turned, this was and that. Up and over and round and through the copper pipes, until soon it was underneath the prison cells and speeding along a magnificent waterway of disgusting and terrible things.It turned around corners, catching the eye of a Small Black Rat, who was stood at the side of the sewers practicing a magic trick with a red ball.

The Rat instantly recognised the sock, and ran after it speedily grabbing it in his mouth. The rat looked frenzied, and raised its head to the sky whilst taking a deep break, before shrieking out a blood curdling squeak, which echoed through the pipes, reverberating through the sewers.

Rats stopped what they were doing, every rat, in the entire sewer, and each one of them raised their heads to the sky and squeaked in unison.

The sound below the ground was deafening. Although in the hustle and bustle of Metrocity not a human soul would hear it.

Not a human indeed, although the already fluffed up fur of Pipsqueak stood up on end even more so, once again making him even more ludicrously large.

He jumped out of Mrs Swan's arms, and sped out of the front door and into the sewers. Pipsqueak knew that he alone may have to be the one to save Denzel, his ringleader.

Chapter 14 - H.M.S Mini Titanic's Sails Again

Milo, grabbed a parent by both arms.

"Come on Mum, Come on Dad. We have to save Denzel."

Before they could complain Milo had dragged them out of the Pink Palace, and back on to the red carpet.

"Come on." Said Milo again, more urgently this time.

"You don't believe he did it do you?" Said Milo frantically.

Again before they had a chance to answer Milo had jumped down into the sewers, and was climbing down the mountain of jewels beneath, towards the abandoned bath tub boat.

Mr Swan smiled nervously at Mrs Swan

"It's quite exciting really, isn't it?"

Mrs Swan took a few seconds, and then a gigantic smile grew across her face.

"Yes Dear, it's probably the most exciting thing I've ever done."

She Jumped into the hole back into the sewer.

"Come on then." Her voice echoed up through the pavement, "If you can't beat them join them, that's what I always say."

Mr Swan Smiled

"Wait up Milo, I'll be back in a few seconds."

He ran back into The Big Pink Palace, staring at PC Sydney Harbour. She was still interviewing Penelope Pompadour, who was milking the whole situation, waving her arms about and weeping into a handkerchief. Sydney's torch lay on a shelf next to her.

Mr Swan slowly crept up behind, and silently grabbed the torch. Sydney didn't notice, but in the many mirrors of the beauty salon, he caught Penelope's eye.

"STOP THEIF!" Cried Penelope, dramatically pointing one of her pink painted talons towards the mirror.

Sydney spun on her heels, but Mr Swan was already running.

"It's for justice." He called behind him, as he disappeared out of the door, outside and back into the sewers.

The light reflected through the diamonds as Mr Swan climbed down the mountain, making the sewers look like they were lit by starlight.

Milo couldn't help but think that it looked almost beautiful, but was concerned as he scanned the area, that Pipsqueak was nowhere to be seen.

"Give back the torch." Cried Sydney down the sewers. "Otherwise you could be in as much trouble as Denzel"

Milo and Mrs Swan were turning the bathtub around and back into the water. Despite the massive mountain of jewels which blocked the way, there was a small stream which went around it.

"It's no good Mum. We are going to have to lift it."

Mrs Swan, gritted her teeth.

"Okay Milo, are you ready we lift on three. One, Two, Three..."

Both Milo and his mother somehow managed to lift the bathtub a little off the sewer floor, and shuffle around the valuable mountain in their way.

Mr Swan was struggling to come down the mountain whilst holding the torch, but knew they would need it if they were to succeed, he was being followed by Sydney who seemed to be speeding up, and becoming more comfortable with crumbling mountain below her.

Penelope's head appeared at the top of the hole.

"Get him." She hissed at the police officer, who looked up and sternly called out.

"Madam please can I ask you to stay outside." Then looked back down to Mr Swan

"I must ask you to stop, Sir, I really don't want to have to arrest you too."

But it was too late.

Mr Swan jumped down from the Jewels and landed splat into the water, his body twisting round, as he gave out a small scream.

Mrs Swan stared at him.

"Are you Okay?" She said grabbing his arm.

Mr Swan was breathing quickly, and limping towards the bathtub.

"I'll be okay. I think I've just twisted my ankle."

He stumbled into the tub, where Milo sat waiting.

"Adios" Shouted Mrs Swan to Sydney laughing loudly as she jumped into the tub, and it sped off down the underground waterway.

Sydney's foot clambered down to the bottom of the mountain of jewels, dislodging a large diamond at the bottom and sending the incredible precious pyramid of gold, diamonds and platinum, tumbling in an avalanche, to the floor. Sydney managed to jump out of the way, but was now stuck on the wrong side of the sewer whilst the bathtub, and Swan family escaped!

The Swans were tossing and turning, this way and that, more eratically than before and with no knowledge of where they might end up. No Denzel to captain the makeshift ship. The pipes seemed to wind with a mind of their own now, and The Swan's had to have been traveling in them for over an hour.

Then a fork in the pipes, the first leading towards beautiful marble tiles, and the other, seemingly forcing them down deeper into the sewers.

Mr Swan and Milo screamed whilst Mrs Swan laughed manically at the back of the bathtub as they approached the centre of the fork and then sped with uncertainty towards the water flying down into the very depths of the sewers.

The tub accelerated down the waterfall, before it reached a free fall. The Swan's had to hold on to the sides of the bathtub, whilst the water sprayed across them from every angle.

It was like a roller coaster ride, as it swung around corners, lurching high into the air, before smashing down into the water again.

"THIS DOESN'T SEEM RIGHT." Yelled Milo at his parents, whilst inhaling a mouthful of the water.

"THIS ISN'T WHERE DENZEL WOULD'VE BEEN TAKING US!" He cried over the bellowing waves around them.

The bathtub groaned as it crashed into the left bank of the pipe, then rolled back towards the right. There was a long crack across the bottom of the tub, and it was starting to fill up with water.

Mr Swan looked down.

"I KNEW WE SHOULDN'T TRUST SOMETHING CALLED H.M.S MINI TITANIC." He frantically shouted pointing at the water which was rapidly filling up the vessel. He was scooping the water out of the bathtub with his bare hands.

Even Mrs Swan's euphoric mood was starting to dwindle, she was looking straight ahead, her eyes wide and, and pointing in front of them.

Milo noticed what she was pointing at.

"DAD THE WATER IS THE LEAST OF OUR WORRIES."

Mr Swan stopped throwing the water out of the tub and looked up, at where Mrs Swan was pointing.

The Bathtub was speeding quickly towards a dead end.

Faster than a train, it sped through the water, they flew through the pipe with nowhere to go.

All three of The Swans took a collective deep breath, closed their eyes and let out a scream, as they crashed into the wall in front of them.

HMS Mini Titanic smashed into several pieces, and The Swans flew into the deep water below. They seemed to be in a huge tank, a gigantic dead end, with no way out, and nowhere to go.

Milo trod water, he was pretty light, and had plenty of practice at his swimming lessons. Mrs Swan also seemed to float almost elegantly at the top of the water. But Mr Swan coughed and spluttered. He was struggling to stay afloat. Unable to kick his legs and writhing in pain from his twisted ankle.

Mr Swan took a huge breath. Staring at his wife and child, and began to sink deep into the dark water. The torchlight fading as he disappeared from view.

Mrs Swan, took a huge breath, and dived under the water. Deeper and deeper she went determined to save her husband.

Milo looked around him to see if he could do anything, literally anything to help. There seemed no way to get out of here, even if his mother was able to get his father back to the surface.

The top of the tank had no hatches.

The walls were entirely solid.

No one knew where they were.

Milo let out scream.

He carried on looking around, there HAD to be a way to escape.

The walls, nothing.

The metal top of the tank nothing.

Wait, the top of the tank seemed to be drifting further away, either it was getting higher, or Milo was getting lower.

Milo looked around him. The walls appeared to be moving up, the top of the tank slowly becoming further and further away.

Mrs Swan resurfaced, holding Mr Swan in her arms. He was unconscious, his body looked limp and heavy.

Milo stared at his Dad, tears in his eyes, then back at the top of the tank in confusion, a slow realisation came over him. The top of the tank and walls weren't moving up, the water was moving down. The tank was draining.

"Hello?" Echoed a woman's confused voice from the outside.

The water had almost all drained now from the tank, yet Mrs Swan still held her husband in her arms. His eyes opened, and water fell from his mouth as he coughed and spluttered.

A small door creaked opened into the dark tank, from the brightness and glare of the lights behind, The Swans' eyes found it difficult to focus on the tiny old woman in front of them.

"Oh Dear, oh dear, oh dearie me. I thought I heard someone screaming in there. I'm Enid, this is Little Acton Water, Can I Help you?"

Chapter 15- Abduction

As the Swan family stumbled out of the huge vat, Enid's eyes were huge with disbelief, and the magnifying lenses made her look a little like an alien, at least that's what Mr Swan thought.

"We come in peace." He groaned, still clinging on to his wife. "That's what us Earthlings always say."

Enid shook her head in puzzlement at the strange man's odd greeting.

"Dad" Whispered Milo frantically under his breath. "She's not an alien."

Mr Swan slanted his eyes suspiciously at her as if to take a closer look, before his eyes coming more into focus.

"OH... I am soooooo SORRY!" Said Mr Swan, pulling away from Mrs Swan and twisting on his bad heel to look at his son, wincing in pain, whilst winking dramatically at Milo.

"Of course you aren't an alien, or a Martian, or any other kind of extra terrestrial." He said forcing a smile at Enid, before adding under his breath "Milo I think she believes me, now call NASA before she discombobulates us."

Milo was strugging not to laugh at his fathers bizarre behaviour, but Mrs Swan looked horrified at her husband. Her mouth was open in surprise, as Mr Swan stumbled around the floor speaking absolute gibberish.

Mrs Swan got her thoughts together, and looking at her husband (who was now looking around the bottled water factory muttering about 'android tech') took a deep breath.

"I must apologise for my husband, he's just had a near death experience, and I think it may have affected his brain a little bit."

Enid gave Mrs Swan a smile, before gently saying.

"Boys will be boys, my Baxter is a big space fan himself."

She took a look around, before bellowing

"BAXTER!"

At the top of her voice.

Milo shot his mother a glance, she gave him a reassuring smile, whilst Mr Swan finally sat down on the floor, and called out in despair to Milo and his wife. "We've been abducted!" He then collapsed, in a heap, on the floor.

 Mrs Swan ran to look after him, she checked his pulse, and that he was still breathing, but it could take some time before he woke up. Milo took the opportunity to tell Enid and Baxter about their day so far, whilst Mrs Swan never left Mr Swan's side.

When Mr Swan finally opened his eyes he was surrounded with people. There was Milo, with a concerned look on his face, his beautiful wife shaking him back and fourth, the old woman, who Mr Swan could now see was 100% human, and someone Mr Swan didn't recognise. A man in glasses, a grey suit and red wiry hair. The man put out his hand, pulled Mr Swan to his feet, and gave a nervous smile

"Hello Mr Swan, I'm Baxter... I've already met the rest of your lovely family. Mrs Swan has just been explaining how you came to end up inside my factory."

Mr Swan's eyes were wide.

"So you know we are running from the police?"

"I do, but they won't come looking for you here, they've already visited us, and it's actually my fault that the pipes led you into the factory in the first place. You see I had to make a little diversion."

"You know about Denzel too?"

"Yes, Milo has told us everything it's very sad that he's in prison, but I think right now it's important to stay put. After all you've done nothing wrong at the moment, except grab a torch, but you don't want to add jailbreak to a reason to have the police after you."

Chapter 16 - Guilty

Sydney looked around the sewers, a little bewildered by the world around her. Penelope stood at the hole above, looking furiously down at Sydney.

"You let them get away!" Penelope yelled down at Sydney. "But worse, You destroyed, my tower of treasure!"

Sydney looked up at Penelope. "Your what?"

"My tower of treasure, my pinnacle of preciousness, my fort of fortune!" Penelope hissed at Sydney. Penelope was furious. But slowly realised she had admitted that the mountain of jewels were hers.

"You mean this was all yours?" Said a bewildered Sydney.

Penelope shifted from foot to foot, before an evil smile grew across her face.

"Yes, of course.I want to build the world's shiniest mirrorball, it's been a project I have been working on for years.

At first just one or two little robberies, nothing anyone would notice, using the sewers as a map of the city. They go everywhere, you can move around almost undetected, slowly building up a secret stash of precious things. I needed a final big job before creating the ultimate mirrorball, and so last night I went on what you are calling The Great Diamond Heist... The heist to end all heists. And I would've got away with it if it wasn't for that disgusting Denzel Sludgeworth!"

Sydney reached for her radio.

"Looking for this?" Called Penelope. "I'm furious, but I'm not stupid. You left it in The Big Pink Palace when you chased after those meddling Swans."

"You must give it back, there is a way we can sort all this out." Sydney called up hopelessly.

"Why of course." Said Penelope, a dirty smile flickering across her face as she dangled the radio over the man hole, before dropping it.

Sydney knew she'd never catch it, and watched in disbelief as the radio seemed to fall in slow motion down into the sewer, before crashing on the pile of stolen jewels, and smashing into smithereens.

"You've admitted the whole thing to me Penelope, you wont get away with this."

"Actually, I think you'll find I will." Penelope started pushing the cover back over the hole. "Because you'll never see the light of another day." Penelope laughed manically at Sydney before the manhole cover fell into place, its metallic thud echoing through the sewers.

It took a good few seconds for Sydney to get adjusted to the darkness of the sewer, now that the natural light from the hole above was blocked.

The odd drip sounded so loud against the silence which filled the echoey tiled caverns beneath Metro City.

Sydney looked down at her broken radio. But it was no good, she wouldn't be able to fix it. She couldn't get up to the manhole any more, and she didn't know her way around the sewer, she would easily get lost in its maze of tunnels and pipes.

Worried and alone Sydney sat down, to try and think of a way to escape. She let out a deep sigh.

Then she noticed, something. A pair of eyes looking at her, then another, and another. Shining in the darkness, staring at her.

Sydney was scared, the darkness and silence of the sewers were unforgiving with her imagination, which automatically suspects some kind of horrific monster.

The sound of scurrying came from the eyes as they swapped places.

And then from out of the darkness came something walking towards her.

"A sewer monster." Gasped Sydney, horrified.

It's eyes were bright and wild, its body was gigantic, and it smelt of marshmallows.

"Wait, you smell of marshmallows?" Uttered a bewildered Sydney Harbour.

The monster revealed itself in the dim sewer lights, it was Pipsqueak.

Suddenly the rest of the eyes moved forwards, to reveal the bodies attached to them, hundreds if not thousands of rats stood behind Pipsqueak, and together they started to squeak at Sydney, before running down the sewer.

Sydney got up and started to run after the rats.

"Wait for me." She called after them.

The Rats carried on scurrying through the dark dingy sewers, Pipsqueak staying with Sydney to make sure She didn't get lost.

The tunnels twisted this way and that, and as Sydney ran further and further into the sewers she felt like they may never end. Then Pipsqueak stopped, as they faced pitch darkness in front of them.

He looked at Sydney, and then ran into the darkness. For a second nothing happened, Sydney was sure that the rats had led her into some sort of trap. Then a light went on, revealing a huge underground cavern painted in yellow and red.

In the centre of the room was a rat, as white as snow, on a tiny bicycle.

Sydney didn't move, she didn't even blink, as the rat slowly started to cycle round and round. Sydney had never seen anything like it in her life before!

This was the rat's plan to free Denzel.

As snowflake cycled round and round, rat after rat jumped on to her tiny furry shoulders creating a rather unbalanced rat pyramid. The final rat to jump to the top of the pyramid, was none other Pipsqueak, holding a grapple made from an old fishing line in his claws.

He swung the grapple around his head, as the rats beneath wobbled precariously, and snowflake frantically cycled round and round in circles. Pipsqueak threw the grapple towards the makeshift sound booth in the corner of the room, which Denzel had made from some old pallets, but Sydney now guessed represented his prison cell.

The grapple took hold, and Pipsqueak jumped, sending the tower of rats toppling into a furry heap on the floor.

Pipsqueak sailed through the air like Spiderman squeaking with glee, before landing in the sound booth, leaving the fishing line hanging down.

Pipsqueak stayed at the top of the line, whilst Presto climbed slowly up it with three of its feet, whilst holding a small cup in the other.

When he finally reached the top he ran from the sound booth he passed the cup to Pipsqueak, before running back down the line again, towards a key from an old tuna can.

Presto gave an impressive flourish with her paws, and the key had vanished. Presto then theatrically gestured to Pipsqueak.

Pipsqueak dramatically raised the cup, to reveal underneath was the key, with a triumphant squeak.

Sydney clapped, and cheered for the rats, who all took a little bow.

"Well it's a fantastic plan." Smiled Sydney. "But you realise I am a police officer... If you can get me out of here, then I can explain that Penelope Pompadour stole the jewels, and there will be no need for a jailbreak for Denzel.

 The rats collectively sighed and looked around at each other a little disappointed. Before whizzing through the sewers again to show Sydney the way to the police station.

Chapter 17 - Freedom

Mrs Swan and Milo sat on the plastic chairs in the Little Acton Water Office, whilst Mr Swan, Baxter and Enid stood. It was dark now, and the electric strip lights flickered and buzzed over their heads. They sat staring at the offices dusty television watching the news. The one story which had dominated the headlines that day. The Great Diamond Heist.

"We now pass over to our roving reporter, Fay Queues, for more on this story."

"Well news has developed here greatly. It seems that the original arrest of Mr Sludgeworth was incorrect, and we are expecting him to leave the police station any minute now."

As if on cue, the door to the police station opened to reveal an exhausted looking Denzel.

"Here he is now." Said Fay, her eyes gleaming with excitement, as she ran towards him.

"Mr Sludgeworth. How do you feel about being wrongfully imprisoned against your will by what we could call an incompetent police force?"

She thrust her microphone at Denzel.

Denzel looked at the microphone, then looked back at Fay, and shook his head.

"I don't mind, I don't 'fink they are incomp-whatever-you-said, they know 'oos done it now, don't they?"

Fay Queue's eyes glistened once again, and she took a deep breath, this was the story she had always wanted.

"Do they Mr Sludgeworth?" she said smiling, with a dazzling aray of far too white teeth. "Do you know who did it? Have you been told?"

Before Denzel got the chance to answer Daphne and Sydney ran out of the police station, grabbing Denzel as they went.

"NO PRESS." Shouted Daphne at Fay Queues, as the three of them slammed into a police car, and zipped off, sirens on. The police car was followed by a hoard of rats which jumped out of the sewers, and scurried behind the car.

Fay turned to the camera.

"Come on." she said excitedly, jumping into her own car. "Get in the passenger seat." She said to the camera, her eyes wide.

Obviously she wasn't talking directly to the Swan family, but it certainly felt like she was. It was like watching a car chase, as the camera bounced up and down, after the rats, who sped after the police car.

They whizzed round corners, over bridges, through red lights, and towards the fashion sector of Metro City.

Back in the office the Swan family sat transfixed.

"I know where they are going." Yelled Mr Swan, as the screen hurtled past an old disused cinema. "They are going to the Big Pink Palace." He turned to look at Baxter and Enid. "Have you got a van?"

Enid Smiled.

"Oh yes! We do, come on Baxter. Lets go!"

And before you knew it the whole family were sat in a Little Acton Water Van, speeding through the night towards the Big Pink Palace.

Chapter 18 - The Mirror Maze

In the dark the Big Pink Palace looked much more like a foreboding fortress than a beauty parlour. It was lit with bright purple and pink lights, which shone across its garish façade, rhythmically swaying this was and that. Outside the police car's blue lights clashed with them as they flashed highlighting a hoard of rats and the news van, which had followed behind.

"I said NO PRESS." Daphne said angrily, slamming the door of the police car.

Fay Queues either didn't hear her or didn't care.

"And so we come to the scene of the crime itself." She said smiling to the camera. "Underneath these very streets lies millions, if not billions of pounds worth of jewellery. The Heist to end all Heists will seemingly end here, at Penelope Pompadour's Big Pink Palace."

Daphne rolled her eyes at the news reporter and made her way up to the door, followed by Sydney and Denzel.

"Listen Denzel." Whispered Daphne. "Go and talk to the news hound, just keep her away from what's really going on."

Denzel winked and smiled, and walked over to Fay Queues, to initiate conversation.

She pushed the door, which opened easily.

The inside of the Palace was dark.

At the back of the Reception area stood Penelope Pompadour. Grinning an evil smile at the Police officers.

"Catch me if you can!" she said, and she pulled a large lever next to her.

Suddenly three things happened all at the same time.

Music blared from the wall speakers, a song called Hungry Like the Wolf, by a band called Duran Duran. It was so loud the police couldn't hear each others voices over it.

The gigantic disco ball started spinning above their heads. Several lights on it, dazzling the Police, and making their vision go fuzzy for a second.

The Mirrors which filled The Big Pink Palace spun in different directions, creating a hundred reflections of Penelope.

"THERES LOADS OF HER!" Shouted Sydney. "HOW DO WE KNOW WHICH ONE TO GO TO?"

"I CAN'T HEAR YOU." Shouted Daphne back at her.

Both Police officers shrugged at one another, and started to slowly make their way forwards towards the centre Penelope.

As they got closer they saw their own reflection too, and realised this was not the Penelope they were looking for.

Suddenly all the Penelope reflections vanished for a brief second and then reappeared, standing very still.

Daphne gestured to Sydney with her hands that they should split up. Pointing Sydney in one direction, and herself in the other.

Disco lights filled the room, as Sydney made her way into the Poodle and Pooch Parlour. It was unrecognisable with the mirrors and the lights, but the devastation caused by Pipsqueak was still across the floor. Three Penelope's stood in this room. Sydney cautiously approached each one, the first and second were both Mirrors, but the third was neither a mirror nor Penelope herself, it was a lifesize cardboard cut out.

As Sydney removed the cutout, every Penelope vanished in the room, Sydney stood in front of the mirror, and suddenly the room was filled with Three Sydneys.

'Clever' thought Sydney 'evil, but clever.'

Daphne was walking towards one of the five Penelope's in her room, and suddenly, all the Penelope's vanished.

Daphne, stared at the room, confused by what had happened and suddenly instead of there being five Penelope's in the room there was now five Sydneys.

Daphne jumped, a little shocked, not expecting to see her partner in the mirrors.

The Sydney's started smiling in the mirror, and checking her teeth, not knowing she was being watched by her superior.

"Sydney, it's hardly the time." Said Daphne under her breath, shaking her head but chuckling to herself.

Both of them realised that if Penelope wasn't in either room, she must still be in the reception area, and they ran out into the main room, to face each other, but no Penelope.

The Song drew to an end, and a huge spotlight, shone up to the ceiling, where Penelope stood on a small balcony, another level in her left hand.

"Not got me yet?" She said cackling with delight.

She pulled the lever and more music belted through the speakers, this time 'Tainted Love' by a band called Soft Cell.

The lighting changed too. No longer did the disco ball create pretty patterns across the walls, but the pair of police officers were plunged into darkness. The walls turned black except for Neon hairdryers, scissors and lipsticks which had been painted on the walls to light up the room.

The mirrors danced into new shapes across the floor, and trap the Police officers in a maze.

"BYE!" Shouted Penelope as she disappeared behind a curtain from the balcony.

Slowly, Daphne and Sydney made their way through the maze, looking for a staircase to get up to where Penelope was leading them.

Outside Denzel was telling Fay Queues about his Rat circus, and the Rats were demonstrating their skills for her. Fay seemed to have forgotten all about The Great Diamond Heist and her big story, and instead was transfixed on the Rats!

Suddenly there was a screech of breaks, and behind them appeared a Little Acton Water Van! Out stepped The Swans, Enid and Baxter.

Milo was the first to spot Penelope on the rooftop.

"Look!" He shouted pointing.

Everyone looked at the roof, to see Penelope standing, next to a small helicopter, its propellers slowly spinning.

"There might still be time to get to her before she gets away in the Helicopter." Said Mr Swan, his eyes wide.

"But there's no way to get up there." said Milo

"There's always a way" Smiled Mrs Swan, determination in her eyes as she stared up at Penelope Pompadour.

Before turning around to her Mr Swan and winking "Isn't that what you always say darling."

Mrs Swan ran round the back of The Big Pink Palace, followed by Mr Swan, Milo, Fay Queues and her cameraman.

Fay clutched her microphone, as she was illuminated by a purple light, and she turned back to her camera.

"Incredible scenes here at Penelope Pompadour's Big Pink Palace, as the story unfolds. Will this normal civilian family be able to thwart Penelope's evil plan. What has happened to the police inside, have they met their sticky end? And where on earth is that music coming from?" (Tainted Love had just finished and the opening bars of Bat Out of Hell by Meatloaf began to blare through an open window!)

"THERE." Yelled Mrs Swan pointing towards a rickety looking ladder, which was clearly designed as a fire escape from the roof.

"There is no chance I'm letting you go up there." Said Mr Swan, "it looks as though it could give way at any second."

Milo looked at his parents, and took a deep breath, before bravely saying "I'll do it."

" No son, you can't." Said Mr Swan filled with concern "What goes up must come down that's what I always say isn't it dear?"

"Yes, Dear." Said Mrs Swan.

"But I'm the lightest, it has to be me." Yelled Milo, pushing his parents out of the way.

Milo started to climb the ladder, but the first rung broke as soon as he put his whole weight on it.

"Well that's it then." Said Milo, there's nothing we can do.

Denzel gave a toothy grin. He was watching something quite different.

"Oh, I wouldn't be so sure."

The family turned to see what Denzel was looking at, to be honest everyone had forgotten he was there. But as they turned they saw the same as him. Climbing up the drainpipe were hundreds upon thousands of rats. And at the very top was Pipsqueak guiding the way.

The helicopter blades were spinning fast and faster, and Penelope let out another cackle, as she jumped into the Helicopter. It started to hover over the roof and the rats started to cling on underneath. Whilst Pipsqueak jumped into the co-pilot seat.

"Urgh, filthy rat." Said Penelope "Get out."

More and more rats clung to the underneath of the helicopter out of the sight of Penelope.

"I said get out." Said Penelope through gritted teeth.

Pipsqueak continued sitting in the seat, buying time, as more and more rats added weight to the Helicopter.

"URGH!" Yelled Penelope as she pushed Pipsqueak out of the helicopter, and sent him tumbling towards the ground. "GOOD RIDDANCE, RODENT." Bellowed Penelope out of the Helicopter, waiting for a splat... But the splat never came!

Penelope leaned out of the helicopter to see tiny claws hanging on to the bottom of the helicopter. To her suprise a whole chain of rats were swaying to and fro, with Pipsqueak holding on at the bottom.

"I'LL SHAKE YOU ALL OFF!" She Screeched, grabbing the Helicopters joy stick and pushing it frantically from left to right.

The Helicopter lurched chaotically through the sky, spinning this way and that, and suddenly seemed to lose control, and tumbled through the sky and towards the ground.

The Swans, Denzel and Fay leapt out of the way, as the rats dived through the sky, letting go off the helicopter. A Scream came from the Helicopter as it descended through the sky, and crashed into the floor.

All was still for a few seconds. All was quiet.

Suddenly the silence was broken by some powerful electric guitar from The Big Pink Palace. And the Stillness was broken by Penelope crawling out from underneath the wreckage.

She got to her knees and then slowly limped towards the small crowd.

"We should help her." Said Milo, walking over to help support her weight. Penelope glared at Milo, but still didn't push him away.

It was a good job he did help her, because as they got towards the small group of people watching, the helicopter burst into flames, an explosion lighting up the skies above them!

Fay turned to the camera.

"Shocking scene's here at Penelope Pompadour's Big Pink Palace."

Penelope glared at The Swans, then at Baxter and Enid, then saw the news camera, and gave the biggest, fakest smile right into the lens, before turning her attention back to the family.

"But there's no police here to arrest me, I could just as easily grab this bag." She grabbed Enid's handbag.

"Take these keys." She pulled the Little Acton Water van's keys out of the bag.

"And get away."

"And no one can stop Me" She started to cackle her evil laugh, but stopped rather abruptly, and looked down at her feet and screamed. She was being climbed on by the rats. They clambered over her feet, up her legs, they jumped on to her body, pushing her down to the ground, in her hair, on her face.

"Get off, Get off of me." She yelled.

Daphne and Sydney appeared from The Big Pink Palace their silhouettes dark in front of the burning helicopter wreck.

"We found our way out of your little mirror maze, and I think you'll find that we ARE here to arrest you." Smiled Daphne, would you like to do the honours, PC Harbour.

Sydney smiled, and took out her handcuffs.

"That'll be the last time you'll ever try and lock anyone in the sewers" she said grinning from ear to ear as she handcuffed Penelope.

Daphne smiled at the Swans and Denzel.

"And you'll be getting the reward for finding the jewels." She said.

"A Reward?" said Milo.

"Yes... 4 Million pounds!" said Daphne. The Swans and Denzel's mouths dropped open.

"Any idea's what you'll do with all that money?"

Chapter 19 -1 Year Later.

I have always wanted to know what happened to the people in the book, after the book finished. And so it is only fair that I tell you.

Penelope Pompadour was found guilty of several crimes, it seemed she had been behind most of the major unsolved criminal robberies since the 80s.

She is now locked up in the highest security prison, in a secret location. No one knows where it is, in fact even the people who work there have to wear a blindfold to get there.

Enid and Baxter closed down the Little Acton Water Factory, and took over The Big Pink Palace, not as a beauty parlour, but instead as an ice-cream parlour, because sometimes a change is what everyone needs. Baxter's office is nowhere near as untidy, and all the staff who once worked at the water factory, now work on the premises making and serving the ice cream!

Fay Queues stopped reporting the news, and is currently starring in 'Celebrity Jungle Quest' a gameshow where TV personalities, try to become more famous than they already are, by competing in disgusting tasks in a jungle.

Daphne Cypher is now the head of the police entirely, and PC Sydney Harbour has been promoted to Detective. They are best of friends and meet up in Tom's Diner every Tuesday evening for pancakes and coffee.

Denzel Sludgeworth invested his money into the rat circus to take it on tour. It became an absolute sell out, and everyone adored the show. Whilst he travelled around the world he met up with other strange, eccentric performers and talented creatures. He asked them to travel with him. Denzel has explored areas of the world that most don't know, or believe exist. He writes to the Swans, almost weekly (if he can get to somewhere to send the letters) The last postcard they got was from The Lost City of Atalanta, where he got into a bit of a scrape with a Merman. But this is a different story for another time...

Mr Swan donated his Million pounds to Raymondo and Newton Springheel. The old cinema has been converted into a wonderful homeless shelter, complete with showers, beds and much, much more, because no one should ever have to be homeless.

Milo Swan isn't allowed to touch his money until he is a bit older, but he has dreams of all the wonderful things he is going to do when he is allowed, and he would especially like to join Denzel for a little while. He got a very cool games console for his birthday which he enjoys playing with his friends from school.

Finally Mrs Swan ended up using her money to set up a charity to help other sufferers with agoraphobia leave the house. Although Mrs Swan managed to overcome her fears and anxiety in a day, it takes other people weeks, months, and some even years. Mrs Swan is glad to help others in the same position she was once in.

Oh and she always, always has milk for her tea.

THANK YOU

A huge thank you to Amy Frost for putting up with me whilst I have sat at the computer letting my mind go wild to write this book, over the past year.

A massive thank you to my parents for always reading to me as a child and encouraging me to enjoy writing and explore my imagination.

Finally thank you to you, the reader, for reading my book... I hope you've enjoyed it!

About The Author

Christopher Frost is an Author, Magician and ventriloquist based in Essex.

He is well known for his family entertainment shows.

For more information see

www.magicfrostie.co.uk

About the Author.

Christopher Frost is a magician, ventriloquist and author.

He lives in Essex with his long suffering wife, Amy Frost, and two children, Zachary and Georgina.

Chris enjoys writing poetry, building lego, and is a flea circus enthusiast.

If you would like to know more about Chris, and his magical antics, shows, or puppets then you can see more about him online.

www.magicfrostie.co.uk

L - #0335 - 080321 - C0 - 210/148/7 - PB - DID3039394